I0779615

CURT

CURT

Kyle Michel Sullivan

KMSCB Books
Buffalo, NY

This book is meant for adults only

979-8-9887577-8-8
(Formerly: How to Rape a Straight Guy)
New edition: 2024
Cover design: JamTheCat
Copyright: Kyle Michel Sullivan

Dedication

To the guys I know who have been through this...
...and those who've done it...

Table of Contents

About the Author

Other Books

(Sample)
The Beast in the Nothing Room

Chapter One

I did it on a bet.

Yeah, I know, I know — that's a stupid-shit reason to do anything, but I was in the mood to do some damage so I figured I'd do it up right. 'Course, it didn't hurt — or help — that I was already pissed at my bitch of a wife from a back-an'-forth we'd had earlier in the day. An' that I had a couple beers under my belt when the idea come up. Shit, more'n a couple. But still all that is, is even MORE of a stupid-shit reason to do anything.

I guess it started out when the two faggots that were buyin' those beers got to yammerin' back an' forth over whether or not any guy is capable of queer sex, no matter how straight he is. They were dumb enough to think I couldn't see what they were up to — usin' this *argument* as a way to see if I was available for one of 'em. Or both. An' how much it'd cost. It's so fuckin' lame. Normally, I can blow that shit off; six years at Mid-State taught me how. But then they got to where they really were snipin' at each other, so there was no way for me to ignore it all. Ignore what they were sayin', I mean. Ignore what it got goin' in my head.

Shit, that makes me sound crazy. I'm not. I swear. But I can see how somebody'd think I was, from some of the crap I spew. Crap that sneaks past that lazy-assed censor in my brain. Sometimes I'll pop off with any kind of shit you can imagine, just to get a rise out of somebody. Kind of a fun game. Sometimes. An' maybe that's what I was thinkin' when I first popped off at Wayne. Nothin' serious, here; just a bit of mind-fuck, y'know? I mean, it's not like I started my day thinkin' I needed to get even with the world one asshole at a time. *Pun intended,* as Lenny'd say. Or even that I really wanted to. But it was just the kind of day — shit, the kind of world I was in — that got me driftin' into somethin' really fuckin' stupid.

But that's how I get, every now an' then. This hard-assed attitude builds inside me where I want to rip somethin' apart — books, clothes, laws, people, it don't matter — an' I can't set myself straight. Can't see the reality of what's happenin'. Can't hear the warnin' bells screamin' in my head till after I'm done an' it's too late. So you see, this really wasn't some snap decision I made after my fifth or sixth brew. It was a slow buildin' ladder of steps that grew up after a few — hell, more'n a few — years of crap heaped on me that got topped off by a few hours of *chit-chat*, as Wayne'd call it.

The day started out with me gettin' pissed at Connie. I mean, she can be a mean cunt when she wants to. Especially when she's on the rag. Oh, she's nice an' sweet an' cute an' all when people are around. She's tiny an' blond, barely comes up to my chin — somebody said she looks like a little bird, a blond sparrow in heels — so no way was she gonna come across as bad-assed to anybody. But when she gets her mouth goin'? Shit, she could make a drill sergeant cry. Still that didn't happen too much; most of the time we got along great. Most of the time.

But that day. That day, she started diggin' at me soon as I got up, bitchin' right an' left about it bein' almost five pm an' shit, as if workin' all night don't mean I can sleep in the day. Now I built up a hide inside the walls so usually I just shrug it off. Or if I'm in a *fuck you* mood, I yell right back at her. Then we crank it up to master-blaster volume an' have a good rip. Call each other every skanky name you can think of. An' wind up in bed, fuckin'. An' those could be some damn good fucks, believe me. Fucks that make you blind in one eye when you cum. Fucks where your nails dig so deep, they draw blood. Fucks where you wet the sheets with your sweat, even on a cold winter night. I think sometimes she got into a rip just to get started towards one of those fucks, an' if that was the case, I could get one goin' just as often as she could. But sometimes...sometimes all I saw was that stinkin' one bedroom rat-trap we had in Hollywood an' the crappy furniture dressed to look new an' the never-endin' boxes of Top Ramen we had to eat instead of real food, an' I just couldn't get up for it an' she'd get t' be too fuckin' much an'...shit, I'd have to bust out an' walk it off or lose it an' turn to my fists.

'Course, I know better than to hit her, now. Last time I did, I almost lost my parole. She had to threaten to take 'em to court or somethin' to make my P-O back off. He'd come by the rat trap to check up on me an' he saw she had a split lip an' he went all ape-shit on me till Connie slammed in.

"I fuckin' had a couple of fuckin' beers an' fuckin' fell out of my fuckin' car!" she screamed at the asshole. "You got a fuckin' problem with it?" One of the few times she used her mouth — an' attitude — for somethin' good. Man, she knew how to make morons like him listen, even when they're tryin' to hand out some shit.

Now understand, ten years of marriage — well, four really, taking Mid-State into account — gets you to where you know the bullshit behind the voice an' can usually figure out what it is they're really pissed about. An' deep down I knew that most of the time with Connie she was really rantin' about some *I'm-The-Artist* director or the usual five-second TV starlet, not about me. She worked on movies as a clothes chick, no, *costumer*, that's it. But this time I just wasn't hearin' anything but her crap, for some reason, so as soon as she got onto the bitch wagon, I could tell where it was headed an' busted out to grab a brew.

Problem was, I left without any cash. Like I had so much. People really ain't so interested in hirin' barely educated ex-cons for those six-figure jobs you hear so much about. So I was cleanin' fuckin' offices after hours for a dyke an' her pussy in a couple downtown office buildin's for about a buck more than minimum wage. An' that wasn't every day; just when they had a big job. An' then they paid me under the table. Meanin' no taxes taken out. No benefits. No nothin'. I didn't have a job lined up for that night an' on top of it, I'd only worked five days in two weeks. Really makes you want to keep on the straight an' narrow, as this ass-wipe of a priest said to me on my way out of County, once. Like he knew dick about how the real world worked. As I finally figured out.

Not that it mattered — me not havin' the cash, I mean. I knew how to get a beer or two without payin'. I was still on this side thirty, sort of blond an' smooth skinned. Well, except for some pimple scars along my chin. But even those made me look younger. An' I got a nice dick. Not huge like a horse, but big enough an' thick an' cut, just like the rest of me. I keep myself in shape, an' I do mean top shape. My gym's my only real money taker — after rent an' food — 'cause if I ever go back inside, it's the best way of lettin' 'em know straight off I can't be punked out. Not easy, anyway. 'Course, I got a week in solitary my first day in Mid-state 'cause some dumb fuck of a Nazi warrior an' his scum decided I was gonna be their bitch. Only reason I kept 'em outside of me was 'cause I near ripped one of the Nazi's ears off with my bare hands. That added to the rep I already sort-of had, so the fuckers left me alone after that, lemme tell you.

So not to brag, but all I gotta do is a few pushups, tuck my shirt in tight, hit Queer Town an' let my muscles do the talkin'. An' if I gotta put up with a few pinches an' grabs in exchange for the quality brew, that's okay. Sometimes I'll even let one of 'em suck me off for a cash outlay. Makes them happy, gets my mind off Connie's crap, an' takes my rocks off in a way that don't mean nothin'. I mean, once you been in jail a few years, you know a mouth's a mouth, don't matter whose it is.

So there I was in this skanky little fag joint in happy hour lettin' this one fat-assed faggot *ply me with alcohol* in the hopes I'll get too drunk to push his hand away when he puts it on my crotch. His problem is, he don't know how much I can drink. Not that I'm a drunk or anything. I lived without it in Mid-state; didn't even think about it. But this queer don't know that, so he's real easy to string along. I'm even thinkin' I'll get a hundred extra since he wants my dick so bad.

Anyway, the fat-assed faggot's name is Wayne. Of course. Half the guys I met in my life named Wayne were queer. Like it's a necessary part of being called that or somethin'. The one thing my mom did right was name me Curt. It's a real name. A guy's name. Shit, it's a whole attitude. Short. Sharp. To the point. No bullshit. Yeah, that's me. Cut the crap an' get to reality.

But back to Wayne. What can you fuckin' say about Wayne? Yeah, he's fat-assed, but it's not like he's a pig or freak or anything. He's just...thick. An' lazy-lookin'. He's got that black an' white hair — salt an' pepper, that's it — an' he's always lookin' at you sidewise, like he's not really lookin' even though you know he is. Which is kind of creepy, y'know. My feelin' was if he'd just take care of himself — like run or swim or do somethin' besides sit in a bar an' try to pick up guys to buy — he wouldn't have to sit in a bar to pick up guys to buy. Guess that's what makes what happened kind of sad. No, stupid. Just fuckin' stupid.

Anyhow, on the other side of me was this skinny little faggot named Lenny. Well, not so much skinny as just plain small. Like that blond-haired guy on that TV show, a couple years back — what's it called? I had to watch it in Mid-State 'cause one of the guards had the hots for one of the girls in it. Some Italian chick who I gotta admit had a nice rack an' great mouth. Anyway, Lenny — if he'd just pump up, a little, an' add a few pounds, he'd come across a lot better'n he did.

Hey. Listen at me. Thinkin' up ways guys can make themselves into better shape. That's what trainers do, ain't it? Maybe I should've been one of them. Show scrawny little guys how to get big an' feel better 'bout themselves, an' all that *bullshit* bullshit so they could go out an' pick up anybody they wanted. Make a hundred bucks an hour, too, on top of workin' out. Hmph, I'd never thought about that, before. But do you need a license or trainin' or...? Or...

Aw, shit, listen at me. Still full of crap. What a dumbass. I keep forgettin', I ain't the kind of guy for dreams like that. They always crash an' burn around me.

Always.

Shit, where was I? Oh, yeah — Lenny an' Wayne. They were tryin' this double-team shit on me. Flankin' me an' keepin' the beer comin' like they're gonna drop a roofie or some viagra on me or some dumb shit like that an' drag me home or out back or to their car to have some fun. Dumb fucks.

Oh, they'd been cool an' shit, at first. They knew somethin' about baseball an' followed the Dodgers. "Though not as much since Mike Piazza was traded to the Yankees," Wayne let slip. Lenny piped in with a sigh that sounded like, "Ah, yes," an' then paused to see if I was so dumb fuck I'd let slip I got the meanin' of it. 'Course that's when I knew for sure they were bullshittin' me, 'cause it's been years since Piazza got shipped out.

I didn't react. Just told 'em I liked the Cubs. I didn't, really; I'm a Dodger doggie, too, but I knew agreein' with guys like that'd just make 'em bolder, an' they were gettin' kind of hands-on, already. No need to rush things; not till I get myself worked up for it.

But somehow they got to bitchin' back an' forth about guys an' sex an' who'd do it an' who wouldn't. They wanted me to think it was all about some football player they'd heard rumors about an' whether he'd do it even if he wasn't into guys if he got drunk enough. But I still figure they started it as a way to see if they could do a double suck-off on me. I'd done that for two-hundred once, but they didn't know that an' I was takin' the attitude that *I didn't do that kind of thing.* Which I thought'd probably get the price up to two-fifty before they were done. But all of a sudden it was turnin' into a real bitchfest. Not as bad as Connie'd been, but not fun. Not what I wanted t' be around. Like I said, it gets rough thoughts goin' in your head.

Anyway, Lenny was swearin' you could get any guy you wanted, in the right place at the right time if you approached him right. An' Wayne was sayin', no way.

"It's a biological thing," he sniped in this snotty queer way he had. "Some men just cannot have sex with men. At all. Others may or may not, depending on where you are in the bell curve."

Which brought a big *Huh?* from me. "And some men cannot have sex with women, period. End of story. It's not a choice to those on the opposite ends of the spectrum."

"Bullshit," said Lenny, snipped, really. Sniped an' snipped; the perfect nicknames for those two. An' he kept on with, "Sexual function is beyond one's control. Period. Researchers are just now figuring out that men have no real say over what their dicks will and will not do. No, seriously!"

I was laughin' at that one. These *researchers* are so fuckin' lame. Posin' questions in blind studies an' expectin' the answers they get're true 'cause the guy doin' the answerin' don't have to tell 'em who he is. Which is bull. Everybody lies, even to himself. Even in private. But I'll tell you one real truth — show me any guy in prison, give me ten minutes with him an' I'll tell you what he can control an' what he can't. I know; I've run my own *tests*.

Like there was this one guy — few years younger than me — wound up in my cell. It was his first time in house an' he was scared shitless some big black fuck'd fuck him. He had reason — he was white an' had a pretty mouth. I even caught some vatos givin' him the look. I figure he played lots of basketball, he had that kind of feel. Those kind of legs. Not sticks like all those tall skinny black guys you see all over the NBA, but shorter an' stockier. Like what you'd see on a local court. Like what's-his-face — John Stockton, who used to be on the Jazz. Yeah, that's it; he looked a little like John Stockton, just not as scrawny.

He stuck pictures of his girlfriend an' a kid he had by some other chick up over his bunk, like he was advertisin' how straight he is. Like it'd mean anything. An' he wouldn't go near anyplace where he could get taken, if he could help it. I heard a couple of guys tried to take him down in the shower an' found out he knew how to fight. Seems that's what landed him in there — beatin' the shit out of some other punk who pulled some crap on him or stole his pot stash or some shit like that; I never did get the story straight. Didn't care if I did, either.

Anyway, I already knew he was gonna be my next mouth. That's all I'd wanted from these punks up till then — just somebody else to do the job instead of my right hand. I figured I'd get him to trust me then make him give me a blow job, an' I'd make him happy to be givin' it 'cause I'd protect his other end. I'd tried fuckin' a guy after a year inside an' didn't really get off on it, but blowjobs? Hey like I said, a mouth's a mouth. So I put out the word. Didn't take long for it to get around that this fresh meat was Curt's so stay the fuck away. Maybe the guys thought he was already lettin' me have at him, even though I wasn't plannin' anything till he'd got to feelin' nice an' safe. Makes it easier. An' nicer.

So we'd been bunkin' for about four weeks an' I was figurin' another week before it was time to break him in, but this one night he felt safe enough to undress where I could see him. An' I finally saw that he had this round smooth bubble of an ass. Like something a fag photographer'd take a picture of an' put in a dick magazine. An' it got me to thinkin' about Connie.

Her hair was the same color as this punk, but I didn't notice it till that night. Her skin was as smooth as his. Nice tight perky little butt an' round tits that were real as real could get. Not big, just right. Shit, I loved suckin' on her tits for an hour before I fucked her. Made her crazy, all set to go before I began pumpin', an' then she'd wrap her pussy around me so tight, it made me gasp an' groan an' pump even harder an' flat out roar when I fired. Shit.

Well...that thought got me goin'. Got me th' meanest fuckin' wood I'd had since I arrived. I couldn't get her out of my mind, an' it was the first time since I'd been in that I couldn't. Shit, my balls were so blue I didn't want to move. But I couldn't lie still, either. Just the feel of my boxers against my skin brought me close to lettin' loose. But no way was I gonna let that happen while this kid was still awake; it might spook him an' make breakin' him in too tough.

So I lay there, as still as I could, waitin' while he did his bedtime thing — piss an' brush his teeth an' comb his hair. He wore this ratty tee shirt an' high school gym shorts to bed, like always. He never said nothin' — shit, I think we said a total of ten words to each other up to that point — just plopped on his bunk an' went to sleep about two seconds after lights out, like he always did. I already had a sock stashed under my pillow, an' it took me about two seconds of pullin' in it to get myself off, all without a sound.

But it didn't work. Not a bit.

Man, this picture of Connie was so hot in my mind that night. I mean, I could just see her. Feel her legs wrappin' 'round me. Feel her hands on my ass pullin' me harder against her. Smell her perfume as I sucked on her tits while I pounded away. Hear her sayin' "Oh, yeah, oh, yeah, oh, yeah," as she used muscles I'd never known chicks had 'fore I met her. I wanted — no, NEEDED to pump my dick into somebody just like I had her, so fuckin' bad, right then. An' I knew jumpin' the gun an' grabbin' a half-assed virgin's blow-job wasn't gonna hack it this time. But like I said, I only fucked a guy once, before, y'know, an' it wasn't all that great. So that's why I'd been okay with blow jobs the two years since that, 'cause they didn't mean anything. Same for my right hand. So really that's all I'd needed. Till I saw that kid's ass. I couldn't kill the image in my brain. An' I wound up with another ragin' boner.

Christ, I'd of killed to have a go with Connie, right then. My hands itched to touch her skin. An' her kisses, just like sex without sex involved — if that makes any sense. Our bodies crushin' like we were tryin' to melt inside each other. Oh, God. I started rubbin' my hands together, soft all over each other like she'd do to get me started, sometimes. Tickle the hair on my wrists. Then the tender spot under the palm of my hand. Then trail her fingernails up along the inside of my fingers. Fuckin' shit, I needed way more'n a memory, right then.

I finally gave in. What the fuck; I knew what to do an' if I closed my eyes real tight, maybe it'd be just like with her. So I pulled off my boxers, slipped from my bunk an' stood there with a ragin' boner, lookin' at him sleepin' there.

He looked even more like a kid, lyin' on his side, mouth open just a little. An' it *was* a pretty mouth. Curved like a girl's, but not in a sissy way. More innocent an' gentle. Then I thought about my little brother. Few years younger than him. Only family I had left.

I hadn't seen him in three years. He'd just about be done with high school. Probably did good; he was a sharp kid. But then...I'd seen other sharp kids crash an' burn an' wind up in here. All it takes is one lousy moment when your luck's lookin' the other way for you to wind up crushed. Like this dumb kid lyin' here. Just one dumb mistake. Not like me. My life's a series of 'em, even up to then. With him, all it took was one...an' then the fucked up *justice system* sent him here. It wasn't right.

Man, I wouldn't want somebody to do to my brother what I was about to do to this guy. An' that kept me from movin'. I dunno how long I stood there, but I was startin' to lose the edge. Startin' to pull back to where another hand-job'd hold me. Take a little longer on this one. A little slower. More mind to it. Fact is, I was about to get back up on my bunk to get started on one when he rolled onto his back an' one of his legs got uncovered. An' it was white. An' smooth. An' almost hairless. An' so much like one of Connie's legs, I dropped on top of him without a thought.

My hand was crushed his mouth before he knew what was happenin', an' I had this plastic fork handle I'd ground down to where you could cut paper with it jammed against his neck. He started to fight me, so I dug it into him. Cut his skin, a little. He stayed still, then.

"Be glad it's just me," I said, real soft an' mean. "I could let a dozen of 'em in here to have you. Even make some stash off it." Then I took my hand off his mouth an' pulled his shorts down from his hips — no, tore 'em. I heard 'em rip an' felt his dick flop against my hand. I jerked it away.

"Don't, man," he was whisperin' over an' over, "please. This isn't my way. I've never done that — "

"Shut up! You say one more fuckin' word, this goes in your

brain. You got me?"

He nodded his head an' the little pussy started to weep like a girl. Shit, I didn't cry when I got it front an' back from three Mexicans my first time in, an' I was lots younger than this little faggot. An' that pissed me off.

He started to roll onto his belly, but I stopped him. I hadn't liked it like that, before, so maybe if I fucked him more like I fucked a girl, it'd be better.

I used my knees to shove his legs apart, then felt around for his hole. He was shakin', he was so scared. An' somethin' stirred behind my heart. I loved it. Loved the strength it gave me. The power. The control. I used my free hand to put his legs up on my shoulders — makin' damn sure the fork was still stuck to his neck — then I put my dick right up to him. He began to struggle, again, but I cut him. Not deep, just enough to let him know I meant it. Then I said, "Don't say a fuckin' word while I'm doin' it, bitch. You yell or scream or let anybody know I'm fuckin' you, you're fuckin' dead."

It was hard pushin' into him, like his ass was frozen shut. I used some spit to wet things up an' still had to work my way in, but once I got the head in, the rest followed easy. He gasped, then grunted an' groaned an' tried to wiggle away the whole time, but I had him too tight. Man, he had to work at not cryin' out. In fact, he wasn't doin' too good at it, so I yanked his shirt up an' rammed it into his mouth an' he bit on that to keep quiet. An' then I got busy pumpin', 'cause I wanted it done quick.

Now I ain't gonna lie to you — workin' myself into him like that an' then fuckin' him — it felt good. A hundred times better'n that first guy. I finally understood why the guys would tell you that your right hand only goes so far. There's somethin' about bein' inside somebody else to get off that adds ten times more pleasure to it when it's what you WANT to do. An' my mind got wrapped up in that, I think. Took me back to the last time I fucked Connie, just before I was busted. An' for a minute, it's like she was there...if that makes any sense. Like...I looked down at him, an' for a second I thought it was her. Guess it was 'cause of the darkness an' shadows an' the little slits of light comin' in from the walkway lights, but I could of sworn it was her. Was her body under me. You see, I...well, his pecs were round an' flat an' solid. I'd even shown him some exercises in the gym that could fill 'em out a bit, build him up some; part of the *trust me* bullshit. But there in the dark they looked a little bit like Connie's tits, swear t' God. I mean, like — like when she's lyin' back an' they sort of flow to the sides. Just not as soft an' — an' shit, I dunno how t' describe it; I just saw her when I saw them. An' all of a sudden, I caught myself suckin' on his tits just like I would've done with her.

You see, this is exactly how I fuck my wife — her legs in the air, inside her, my tongue on her tits an' me pumpin' away. Slow at first, then faster an' harder as we got closer to the jolt. She said I could make her cum more than any guy she knew, an' I know she wasn't bullshittin' me 'cause she's a talker when she's gettin' fucked. Maybe that's why I liked the oral thing with my punks up till then; I don't want the little fuckers yappin' or moanin' or cryin' or anything like that. Maybe that's really why I jammed this pussy's shirt in his mouth — so he'd just keep him from sayin' anything.

Didn't do a hell of a lot of good. He whimpered the whole time I was doin' him. Not that it made any difference, 'cause I was so lost in it. I mean, you'll never know how good it felt. How much it was like bein' with Connie, again.

Then I shifted from one tit to the other an' he lost it, for a second. He tried to twist away, but I cut him a little more an' he stopped. An' I kept suckin' on him just to show him who's boss.

Then I felt somethin' bump up against my gut that freaked me out. He was gettin' a fuckin' woodie! I couldn't fuckin' believe it. He couldn't either.

I stopped an' pulled back, a little, an' glared at him. "What th' fuck? You a fag?"

"No," he whispered. "I've never. Never."

"Bullshit, bitch," I whispered back. "You like it. I can feel how you like it."

"No, man, it hurts," he grunted. "Please, just get it over with."

So I laughed an' began strokin' into him slower an' deeper, makin' him really feel it. Try an' tell me what to fuckin' do, the little bitch. He almost sobbin' as he kept beggin' me to end it. An' I just kept on an' on. An' his dick kept callin' attention to itself. I slapped it aside a couple of times but it kept poppin' back, bigger than the time before. So I did somethin' I'd never done before — I grabbed it. Grabbed his fuckin' dick. Yanked it out of the way an' kept pumpin' into him. An' the way he moved around as I fucked him made it seem like his dick was fuckin' my hand. But I didn't let go.

To this day, I dunno why I kept hold. I'd never thought about hangin' onto a man's dick, before, but the way I could feel it bouncin' around against my belly...feel his balls rubbin' my pubes...feel his tits get as pointy as Connie's, almost...it made me notice it more an' more. So I just put my free hand around it an' held onto it like I owned it. Like he was completely was mine an' that proved it.

He tried to stop me, but I smacked his face. Then I grabbed even harder on him. Crushed my hand around him, like I was gonna tear it off. He sobbed even harder an' begged me not to. Begged me to leave him alone. An' then he started to struggle an' I got even more into it.

I fuckin' owned him, right then. I was the boss, an' nothin' he did was gonna stop me or slow me down. The more he fought, the more I felt in control. An' then he jolted. He almost pulled himself off me, but I had too good of a hold on him...an' then he bucked me, again. Rammed himself harder onto my dick. An' he shot all over my hand. All over himself. An' I felt his ass tighten around me in a way that made me want to stay inside him for-fuckin'-ever, it felt so...fuckin'...good...an' then I let loose inside of him. Over an' over an' over. It made me weak, almost black out. I felt it on every square inch of my body, from my balls to my heart to straight down my legs, just like I had with Connie the first time. An' I didn't want to move...even as I kept slippin' in an' out an' in an' out to extend the screamin' goin' on behind my eyes.

Holy fuckin' shit.

This is gonna sound weird, I know, but that first time — the first time I got off in a guy like that — it was like the first time I did coke. Swear to God, this sense of peace flooded over me an' shoved aside everything — *everything* that I had in my head. I went blank. Lost all control an' loved lettin' it go. Felt every part of my body join in the joy of what I'd just done. I didn't get that even the first time I fucked Connie. Hell, the first time I fucked a girl, period. It was like my whole body started to float inside my skin. Like my brain wasn't attached to my mind, just to my flesh. This guy I met outside once told me the French call it *the little death*, an' now I knew what he meant. An' I already knew I'd have killed to get it, again.

I don't remember stoppin' or pullin' out of him; I just remember floatin' back to earth to find him lookin' at me in shock. I made damn sure all he saw was me smilin' back at him. But to be honest, now that I was comin' down off that high, I was really shook up. I'd enjoyed it too fuckin' much. First time I really fuck a guy an' it makes me feel better than when I'm with my wife? It fucked with my mind, I'm tellin' you; but I didn't want him to see that. So I pulled back an' used his shorts to wipe myself off.

"You were good," I said, keepin' my voice even an' calm. "You keep quiet about it an' I'll be the only one who gets you while you're in. You let anybody know I did it? You'll get ten guys a night up your ass, an' one of 'em's sure to have AIDS. So play it smart."

Then I crawled back onto my bunk an' faked like I was asleep. I knew he wouldn't pull nothin' on me, but I played it safe, just in case...listenin' for him to make any kind of a move. But all he did was stay in his bunk, breathin' hard, probably thinkin' 'bout that I'd said. What he'd done. There wasn't another whimper out of him. The next mornin', he acted like it'd never happened.

So did I. It was better'n thinkin' 'bout what I'd felt with him. Better'n facin' up to how great it'd been. An' what that'd mean to me.

I had him in my cell for the whole eight months he was in — he got an early out — an' I fucked him every other night. I made him shoot every time I wanted to, too. Not every time; just every time I *wanted* to. To show him who's boss. It was too fuckin' cool. Gave me this feelin' of total control, decidin' which night I'd get him off an' which I wouldn't; the nights I decided not to, I'd put him face down on his bunk to fuck him. Messed with his mind, too, not knowin' which night he'd wind up on his back or on his belly. 'Course, none of those fucks were as good as that first one, for me, but a couple got close.

Funny thing is, it got me to wonderin' if it was just him who got off on bein' fucked, so once he was gone, I tried it out on any other guy who crossed my cell or I took a likin' to. Didn't matter if he was spendin' his first night in or was a third-striker, if I wanted him, I took him the way I took that kid — legs in the air. An' lemme tell you, most of th' little fuckers did the exact same thing while I was fuckin' 'em. All but a few, an' all but one or two of them still got wood; but for some reason, the non-woodie guys got me to fire faster than the others so I guess I didn't have the time to make my stuff work on them.

Anyway, that's how I knew the skinny-assed faggot's line wasn't exactly bullshit.

I knew exactly how to rape a straight guy.

An' I was findin' I kind of missed it.

An' that thought really spooked me. I mean, I'm straight, y'know. Only time I ever fucked guys was in Mid-State, so that don't count. Not really. It's prison an' you do what you gotta to fill the need. But to miss it? To wish you were still doin' it? That...that was freaky. Stopped me cold. Made me wonder if I oughta just drop the brew an' walk. To get away before I started thinkin' too much an' got myself back in prison. But the brew was a cold one an' the faggots weren't ready to reel in, yet. An' I wasn't really set to face Connie. So I blew it off, smirked at

Wayne an' sneered, "You don't know what the fuck you're talkin' about."

Wayne looked at me like I was scum an' nodded his thick faggot head and sneered, "An' just who're you — *Masters an' Johnson?*"

I thought about punchin' his faggot teeth down his faggot throat, for a second, but I knew that'd kill the beer run an' probably land me back in jail since I was still on probation. So I just got real close to him an' whispered, "I don't know fuck about this *Bastards an' Johnston* shit, but I *do* know what happens to a guy when I fuck him — he gets hard an' he cums. Every time." Yeah, I know, I know — it was bullshit. But hey — it never hurts to build up what you can do, not when you're advertisin'.

I must of said it meaner than I meant to 'cause Wayne got too quiet. Like I'd just told him I was gonna cut off his balls, or somethin'. He wasn't so gung ho on gettin' hold of my dick, anymore.

But Lenny-boy, his eyes were on fire. He leaned over an' said, "How do you know? Have you done time?"

I took this long dramatic pause then nodded an' said, "Twice. Once in a county jail. Once at Mid-State."

"Were you raped in prison?" he asked.

"Do I fuckin' look like some faggot could fuck me if I didn't want him to?" I sneered, then I winked at him. He was hooked. He'd pay me three hundred easy to hold him down an' tear off his undies an' ram my dick up his ass. Little pussy.

Wayne had to sneak over to the other side of the bar to get his voice back. "Okay, so you had a few experiences in prison. It's different, in there. Men don't have any other outlet."

I laughed. "You been watchin' that piece of shit *Days of our prison lives* on fuckin' HBO, ain't ya? Connie used to watch it to try an' figure out what I was goin' through. It's so fuckin' pathetic. Like some cornball out-of-touch 'artiste' knows the first fuckin' thing 'bout how life really is inside."

"Connie?" Lenny asked.

Oops! Shouldn't of dragged her into it. So I smiled an' said, "My ex. Dumped me when she found out I'd...oh, done it with somebody besides her. An' my right hand."

"I don't believe it," said Wayne. "Maybe you forced yourself on a couple of fresh kids, but that doesn't mean anything in the realm of empirical research."

"Speak English, you fuck," I said.

"He said your experiences don't count — "

"I know what he fuckin' means," I snapped. "I ain't a retard. But he's usin' fancy words to hide the fact that he's full of shit. All of it's full of shit. *Empirical* research. That's some computer wuss goin' out an' askin' questions of all these guys an' decidin' he knows what the fuck he's talkin' about, even when another wuss'd ask the same questions of a bunch of different guys an' come up with a different answer. You wanna know what my *research* told me? When I fuck a guy — don't matter if he's queer or straight or old or young, don't matter if I grab him at night or in the day, don't matter if he knows me or never seen me before, don't matter if he trusts me or tries to keep away from me — when I get my dick up his ass, I can make him hard, an' I can get him off. An' I do it just to fuck him up."

"Pun intended?" Lenny snickered.

Well...no, but I had to give him props for noticin' it. An' a chuckle. Guess I can be funny even when I don't mean to be. But ol' Wayne, he wasn't done, yet.

"Oh, please," he said. "It's impossible. Some men would be too afraid to experience even an erection, let alone an ejaculation."

"An' just who told you that?" I asked. "Newsweek?"

Wayne gave me this look back — swear t' God, if we'd been in prison, I'd of punched him. It was sort of an *I know what the fuck you're up to* look that gets guys knifed. It must of popped out without him meanin' it to, 'cause a second later it was gone an' this *whatever you say* kind of manner took over with him. But it set off this bell in my head, not loud but there. An' all of a sudden I'm wonderin' if these guys think they can get me drunked up an' back to their place an' used like some piece of shit whore they'd conned into comin' home with 'em. Maybe they'd even grabbed a guy off Santa Monica an' used him. Maybe that's what all this bullshit chit-chat was really about — checkin' to see just what they might be able to get away with, or not. I mean, I know it's happened.

I met this one guy at Mid-State, he did it to a few fags over in Houston. Grabbed 'em off the street in the queer district, tied 'em down in the back of his van an' fucked 'em, then dumped 'em out a few blocks away. They never got a good look at him; all they usually had was the color of the van. An' even when one or two of 'em told the cops, they never really came lookin' for him. Typical. If you ain't part of middle America or rich out the ass, cops don't give a shit about what kind of shit happens to you. It means too much trouble for 'em an' they got troubles enough to deal with. Just ask a cop; he'll whine for hours 'bout how much crap he's gotta put up with, like nobody's got it worse than him. Selfish fuckin' babies.

Anyhow, the guy didn't get caught till he pulled it on some fag while he was in San Francisco. He was seen kickin' this beat-up half-naked guy out the back door of his van an' was chased down by a bunch of pissed off queens. In drag! Even then, he figured the only reason he got put away was 'cause the guy he fucked's dad was one of those *I'm proud of my gay son* types...an' was a judge. No cop or D.A.'s gonna piss off the man who might handle their next case. So he got *two to five* an' has to register as a sex offender for the rest of his life.

"Like that means shit," he told me. "If this'd been Texas, I'd have got off with probation, at worst. An' you think when I go back they're gonna give a shit what I do to a bunch of queers? Shit, no. Not with Republicans runnin' the fuckin' state."

I hear he got out six months ago. Wonder if he's back in Houston?

But knowin' that guy — an' keepin' my distance from him; not so much 'cause I was afraid but more 'cause I just didn't want the trouble his kind of shit brings — it got me to thinkin',

Maybe they really think they're gonna pull this crap with me. Maybe that's really what this is all leadin' up to. If not that, somethin' like it. It'd be funny to see what'd happen if these two middle-aged faggots tried that shit. An' maybe a little fun. See who's really in control here. See what happens when they find out I'm on to their crap. Okay, fuckers, I figure that's a game I can play. Shit, I *know* it is.

That's when I smiled an' looked at Lenny an' said, "Fuck, ol' Wayne ain't much fun, is he?"

"It's been a rough year for him," said Lenny. "He'll loosen up with a couple more screwdrivers." Then he gave me a look an' added, "Of course, we have the makings for all kinds of drinks, at home. It certainly wouldn't take up so much of our ready cash."

I got the hint. *We'll buy you drinks as long as you want, but if you want some money from us, there won't be as much left.*

So I smiled an' gave off a good long stretch that showed off my pecs an' shoulders an' said, "I don't like silly drinks. All it takes is a decent beer in the fridge to make me happy."

"You like an ice cold Beck's?" he said. An' that was the magic word — Beck's. Ol' Lenny went in for the kill an' got lucky. That's when I decided for sure, *Let's see what happens with these two fucks.* So I smiled at him...an' then at Wayne. An' he sort of smiled at me, an' all three of us left.

Lookin' back — I could tell, even then, I wasn't all that up on joinin' 'em. The little bells were still chimin' in my brain, givin' off the idea that I was makin' a mistake. That I oughta go home to my wife, get a good rag goin' an' wind up fuckin' her. An' Connie, she had a lot of good things about her. I mean, it ain't many chicks'll stick by you through six years in prison. She even got me some jobs on sets — carpenter an' crap like that — but then things'd quieted down an' she had to fight to get jobs for herself. Oh, she could've made it okay if she hadn't had this big dick of a husband draggin' her down, but she never said nothin' 'bout me gettin' lost. Except when she was pissed, an' even then it was more like, *pull your own weight, asswipe.* So I had an idea, even then, I was tossin' aside somethin' I really needed — no, wanted. But like the big dumb log-headed idiot I am, I just sort of drifted along with ol' Lenny an' Wayne, sniffin' after a brewski an' a couple of bills. Driftin' just like I had my whole life. Driftin' straight into hell.

What a fuckin' idiot.

Chapter Two

I walked with them over to Lenny's place, that turned out to be Wayne's, too. They shared this townhouse or duplex or whatever you want to call it in West L-A, where the parkin's the worst an' parkin' enforcement's mean as a gangbanger after a week in solitary. It wasn't a fancy place on the outside — I mean, from what I could tell in the dark — but even with the nearest street lamp half a block away an' the night clouded over, I could see they kept it up. The two inches of front yard they had was covered with roses an' this thick kind of ivy-like stuff reachin' over the cement blocks beside the steps an' up the cement walls. The place was square with a flat roof — not good in LA in the summer; makes the house hotter — an' a yellow light was on by an iron gate of a door. The windows had bars over 'em, too. Reminded me of my six years at Mid-state, though this was a little cozier lookin'.

Inside, it was all done up in the best queer taste — big solid antiques all over *draped* with pillows an' afghans an' flowers in vases or plants in pots, knickknack shelves an' big-framed pictures coverin' *tastefully subdued* wallpaper, windows that had what Connie once told me were *treatments* to give them *character* — making it just scream *faggot hole*. Most of the pictures were of smooth naked guys posing like girls with pouty lips an' arms stretched back. Like any real man'd think that's sexy. Made me want to laugh an' puke at the same time.

What is it with fags buyin' into everybody's idea of what a fag is like? Girly shit everywhere that no girl'd have in her place. Connie's big into nice things an' decoratin' an' makin' a place to her taste an' all, but she never had crap like this around her. She went for clean an' simple an' easy to keep up an' comfortable, things that make a room a home an' not some overdone shit you find in a decorator's window. But these two? They're the type that gives all fags a bad rap an' keep it goin'.

I knew a couple of fags at Mid-State who were as much like a guy as me. They were in for drugs — possession, I think, but it might of been more — an' didn't seem all that bright...but hey, look at me — I ain't exactly a poster boy for higher education. But these guys, they were okay. Couple of *regular* mutts, not overbuilt, not smooth skinned, not bitchy or faggotty, just a couple of...well, I guess they sort of fit into the stoner dude life an' they just got off on each other. That don't mean they couldn't fight if they had to. One of 'em knew Aikido an' showed it off on a couple of vatos who thought he'd be funny on his tummy; the other just fought like a street punk, mean as shit an' nowhere near as fair. You could respect both of 'em, even if they did like to suck dick.

I figure there's lots more like 'em all over the place. But since all you see on the TV an' in movies an' in the news an' shit is the weird ones, you think all of 'em are weird. An' guys like Lenny an' Wayne buy into the weirdness, too, an' keep it goin'...just like most of the guys in queer town.

But at least Lenny made good on his word — a dark ice cold Beck's. I dunno what it is, but black German beer makes me happy. An' horny. Maybe it's the bite to it. How it don't just pretend it's beer, like that piss-water from Colorado, but first it lets you grab it an' then it grabs you right back, like it's sayin', *I ain't gonna play around, asshole; I'm the real shit.* I once thought that I wouldn't mind goin' queer if I met a German faggot who owned a good brewery an' was built good an' liked it up the ass. But most of the Germans I've seen look like sneaky rabbits, an' I hear none of 'em's cut, so I guess that leaves that out. Too bad, in a way.

I took a long drink of the beer an' flopped onto a big-backed chair. No sense in lettin' myself wind up on the couch too quick, not till after the third or fourth Beck's. Maybe. I was already buildin' a little buzz from the Heinekens at the bar, though they don't really count as bein' beer 'cause they brew 'em here in the states an' make 'em half what they are in Europe. I know 'cause this one faggot I let have my dick had some direct from — where'd he say? Denmark? Holland? — but I'd had three or four, so I was gettin' in the mood.

Lenny an' Wayne sat on opposite ends of the couch, both lookin' at me an' tryin' to be cool, but I could see their eyes dartin' from my face to my crotch to my pecs to my legs then back to my face. An' I played 'em, no question. My jeans were tight an' I wasn't wearin' my briefs; I took 'em off last time I hit the john. An' I kept my legs apart, not so wide it looked like I was tryin' to be hot but just wide enough to let 'em get a good idea of what they could have. I was figurin' I'd get maybe two-fifty, three-hundred from 'em an' an encore at some later date, the way they were droolin'...Lenny way more than Wayne.

We bullshitted some — about how good Beck's is an' how long they'd had their joint an' how they thought of themselves as the West Coast *Felix an' Oscar,* but out of the closet. Wayne had to explain to me about *The Odd Couple* since I never watched TV outside prison. Never paid attention to reruns. He did it like some bitchy old maid schoolteacher would; "Well now, little boy, this is a story about two middle-aged men who live together, and who are real opposites, in everything, and how they get on each other's nerves, just like real people do," an' yap yap yap, just like a Chihuahua. What did Lenny call him? Condescending. Yeah, that's it.

Thing is, Wayne *did* look a little like Jack Lemmon. I'd seen him in this old movie Connie made me watch, which I didn't mind so much 'cause I've always had the hots for Shirley McLaine; she looked like she could handle herself. Anyway, Wayne had that same fussy directness an' the same kind of hair an' sort of the same chin, even if he was a good forty pounds heavier.

Now I could tell Lenny's got all these questions he wants

to ask me 'bout what happened in prison, but he kept dancin' around 'em, like they were snakes tryin' to bite him. It was Wayne who finally gave up on the bullshit.

"Tell me something, Curt," he said, leanin' forward just a bit, his eyes lookin' straight at me. "Have you really raped a man?"

Lenny rolled his eyes at that an' sneered, "Of course he has, twit. He's been in jail. I mean, look at his tattoos."

"Porn stars have the same kind of tattoos, Lenny," he sniped back, "but they haven't necessarily forced a man to have sex with them."

Porn stars? Fuckin' asswipes that let themselves get fucked for cash on video? That got my back up. I glared at Wayne as I said, "You think I do porno?!"

He backed down a bit...but not much. "I don't know," he said. "That's why I'm asking."

That really pissed me off. I swallowed the rest of my beer an', since Lenny's was on the glass coffee table between us, I helped myself to his. He let me. Then I leaned forward an' looked straight into Wayne's eyes an' said, "I did six years at Mid-State. For drugs. They don't allow private visits with your wife, an' your right hand only goes so far. You do the math."

"But c'mon, there are other possibilities," Wayne said. "Gay men who are willing to have sex in exchange for — "

"They give you AIDS," I said.

"Oh, now that's insulting!"

"That's the truth, you fuck!" I snapped. "Most fags in prison got there 'cause of drugs — usin' 'em, whorin' for 'em, stealin' to buy 'em, that kind of shit. If they ain't got AIDS from gettin' fucked, they got it from a needle. Only dumb fucks do it with them. Then those dumb fucks take it home to their wives an' girlfriends, or they gang-bang a guy an' give it to him an' he takes it home when he's let out. Smart guys get fresh clean meat, straight guys in for the first time. Smart guys keep 'em to themselves as long as they can."

"And you're a smart guy?" Wayne asked.

I just sneered at him. "I don't think I'm all that fuckin' dumb."

"How many times have you been in?"

"Why?"

"Just curious. You sound rather experienced for someone who's only been to prison once."

Shit, the fucker was payin' attention. An' it was makin' me feel...well, feel weird. Like they wanted me t' tell 'em more than I really wanted to. But it also felt...I dunno, felt good to be talkin' to somebody besides Connie. Somebody who acted like they gave a shit, even if they really didn't. Connie, she'd act like she's listenin', but after a while I figured out she was really thinkin' 'bout somethin' like the costumes she had to pull together for nothin' for some low-rent movie she was workin' on, so I stopped tryin' to talk with her. But Wayne — it seemed like he wanted to know. Really wanted to. An' not just to be nice, y'know? Or for *chit-chat*.

Then I got the idea there was somethin' more goin' on here, somethin' I couldn't quite figure out. An' I remembered I got the same vibe earlier from him, so it made me want to be careful with how much I *did* tell him.

I must of taken longer than I figured to answer, 'cause Lenny added, "Well, are you up for a third strike?"

I shook my head. "My first time, I was a kid. They wiped it clean when I met probation. Then came Mid-State."

"Were you raped?"

That question came at me, low an' quiet, from Wayne. Now I remember I'd already told these two I wasn't, so now I knew they didn't believe me. But I wasn't gonna tell 'em anything else. Problem is, he got my mind ripped back to my first time inside.

I wasn't even eighteen. Just a dumb-shit kid who got too deep into pot an' wound up havin' to pay off his dealer by doin' some transactions in home room. I got narc'd out by this little fucker named Anthony on the school's varsity baseball team. Little *Mister Born Again* Boy Scout bought a joint off me an' turned it over to the principal, who turned it over to Vice, who turned me over to the County Jail.

Now, I'd never been in trouble, before — I mean, not where th' cops had come down on me — so it looked like it was just gonna be a smack the wrist time for this one. They put me in a holding cell an' called my mother to come bail me out.

Good ol' mom did just like she always did — she bailed. Told 'em to make me take care of it, myself; that she was *tired of dealin' with me*. Like she ever had really dealt with me. Fuckin' cunt. She could get stoned an' blasted an' knock me around — till I got big enough to knock her back — an' leave me to fend for myself most of my life, but th' second I get in copland trouble, she figures, *Well, he sneaks out at night an' gets stoned an' had a fight or two an' my new husband doesn't like him, so he's on his own.* I hate her fuckin' guts, an' when I finished with that stint, I split. I've only seen my brother, since.

So there I was, this scared punk kid caught dead to rights an' no one backin' me up, with a public defender who had a thousand other cases to follow. He told me to plead guilty an' he'd try to get leniency. I got lucky; the prosecutor offered a plea bargain of six months in county, an' the judge said that if I was good, they'd wipe the slate clean. So in I went.

Since this was my first time in, I didn't know what the fuck was goin' on, but that didn't stop the guards from actin' like I should. They treated me like I was the devil's disciple or some such shit. Anyway, I got transferred to a long-term wing an' made it through bookin' an' th' mug shot, okay. But then they strip-searched me. An' then the pig that was doin' it pulled on some rubber gloves an' shoved his fingers up my ass. Didn't say a fuckin' word about what he was gonna do, first; he just poked 'em in. I jumped an' kicked him off me an' the other guards smashed me 'round the room for a few minutes. Then they shoved me over a table an' held me down an' let th' fucker dig up inside my ass lookin' for I don't know what. When the finger-fuckin' was done, he told me to wipe my ass an' get dressed. I did. Then I started cryin'. Swear to God, I couldn't help myself — I just started blubberin'.

Well, that made the fuckers laugh an' sneer. An' this one motherfucker got down in my face an' smiled an' said, "You think you're sorry now? We're gonna show you what sorry fuckin' means, cocksucker. We're gonna teach you how to do time."

Then they took me way in the back an' down this block of cells. All of 'em were packed with guys who looked like they could rip your heart out with their pinkies. The place reeked of piss an' sweat, like six-year-old laundry, an' the prisoners whistled an' called out to me as I was escorted past. I was really gettin' scared that I was gonna wind up in some cell with a dozen black guys an' they'd spend the night beatin' me up for bein' white. I had no idea what could really happen. Then they stopped before this one that had two sets o' bunk beds...an' three gang-banger *Latinos*.

One of the guards, this big fat ugly Mex named Martinez, shoved me in an' slammed the gate shut. Then he smiled an' said, "Have fun," an' he an' the other two guards walked away.

Those motherfuckers knew what was gonna happen. No question in my mind. They did it to punish me an' his last crack was to let the vatos know it was okay. 'Cause soon as they left the floor, my fuckin' cell-mates were surroundin' me, askin' me questions like, "What you in for, ese?" an' "You a maricon, pendejo?" an' shit like that. I couldn't get away from 'em.

Now I wasn't exactly a skinny-assed kid, back then. I'd been half-back on the football team a couple years — when things were lookin' up for us, just after mom got married — an' I pumped a little iron, though nothin' regular. An' I'd been in enough fights to know how to defend myself. But that don't mean shit when you're faced with three guys who've had more fights in a month than you had all your life.

I tried to stay calm, tell 'em everything was cool, that I was down with their deal. But they kept circlin' me an' yankin' me by my chin to make me look at 'em an' goin' chest to chest with me. Then one grabbed my ass an' said, "Hey, I bet you a faggot." I clipped him with my elbow an' that's th' only real hit I got in.

They didn't punch me, back; they didn't need to. They just took hold of my arms an' legs an' carried me over to a bunk bed.

Next thing I knew, I was bein' held face down on a lower bunk, one vato sittin' on my back, another one on my legs. I was yellin' an' callin' for the guards, even though I knew they wouldn't come, 'specially since the rest of the floor was yellin' along with me. Then this one chunky asshole named Paco slapped me a few times an' told me I was gonna suck them off, told me that's all they wanted. An' he told me that if I bit any one of 'em, they'd cut my balls off. He showed me a shiv to prove he could do it. Then he pulled out this thing that looked like an eyedropper an' was about th' same size as one till he yanked it to where it was hard, an' put it up to my mouth.

"C'mon, puta," he whispered. "Take it. Do it right."

An' I did.

I took it.

That's how scared I was. An' I gagged as I did it, an' not just because of what he was doin' to me but also because he was so...fuckin'...dirty. Stank of piss an' shit an' head cheese. I choked on it as he shoved it in an' out like he was fuckin' my face. An' when he came, I almost blew chunks. Then his buddies did the same thing to me, all of 'em so fuckin' much like Paco, I couldn't tell 'em apart. Then they called me a fuckin' puta, slapped me around a bit an' flopped on a bunk to talk an' play cards.

My brain went dead. I couldn't believe what I'd just done, all without any real fight. Somethin' I'd never of thought could happen to me. But it had. An' I couldn't even think about it. I just lay where they left me an' my mind stayed blank. I'd of lay there all night but after about an hour, Paco slapped my ass an' told me it was his buddy's bunk, so I had to climb onto a top one. I spent the night starin' at the ceilin', not thinkin' or anything. I felt filthy an' sick an' I was shakin' an' I hated my fuckin' mother so fuckin' much, right then, if she'd come t' get me I'd probably have killed her. I didn't sleep a wink.

But that wasn't the worst part. That came the next night,

after lights out. That's when Paco an' his buddies yanked me off my bunk an' slammed me against the wall. Then Paco started rubbin' my ass an' tellin' his buddies how nice an' round it was. He said it in Spanish, not realizin' I knew some. Just enough to figure out what he's sayin'.

I tried to get away from him, but his guys held me too tight. So I said, "C'mon, man, I did what you wanted, last night. So leave me alone. Please, man...please."

Paco laughed an' yanked my pants down to my knees, then he pulled my briefs down. Then he rubbed his hands over my skin, sayin', "He's sweet. Smooth as my bitch's ass. An' white." An' then he rammed himself inside me. No warnin', just somethin' that felt as big as a fuckin' banana suddenly inside me.

I felt like I was being ripped in half, it hurt so fuckin' much! I screamed, I know, but I don't remember for how long. All I can tell you for sure is, he kept pumpin' into me an' it kept hurtin' an' his buddies kept gigglin' about it for what seemed like hours before he stopped. Then the others fucked me, each one of 'em. An' when they were done, they said I was theirs. Let everybody in the jail know it. I didn't have the first fuckin' idea what to do, so I let 'em get away with it. An' I kept tellin' myself I could hold out till my time was up.

But after a couple weeks, Paco got sick of me an' started tryin' to pass me around for cigs an' dope. By that point, I wasn't dumb-fuck enough to let 'em turn me into a jailhouse cunt, so I let slip to the whole wing how *Paco'd slapped me with a dose of herpes*. Nobody wanted to even try me out, then. He got pissed as shit when he found out, an' him an' his vatos came close to killin' me, that night — punchin' me an' kickin' me an' throwin' me around. I let 'em till they threw me on the bunk an' started rippin' at my pants. I was ready for 'em, this time. I'd hidden a plastic fork behind the bed. I got real still, like I'd given up was gonna let 'em butt-fuck me, again. Then just as Paco was ready to plow into me, I jolted an' kicked his amigos off me an' swung the fork at Paco. I nearly ripped his balls off. Then I used it to hold his vatos back till the guards came. They didn't have much choice, that time, he was screamin' so fuckin' loud. The second I heard 'em gettin' close, I broke the fork, chucked it down the toilet an' flushed.

Shit, I couldn't tell who was more pissed — the vatos or the guards cause they couldn't prove I had a weapon. They threw me into a basement cell for a week, anyway, till they could sort their shit out. Then I got released after the infirmary doctor confirmed I was just defendin' myself against *a brutal sexual assault*, an' they shifted the vatos to another cell block. I got even smarter an' told this guy from that block who was in the infirmary, that Paco's buddies loved to suck me off as Paco raped me. I hear they really *did* get to where they did, before long. An' the best part is, word got around I ripped Paco's balls off with my bare hands, so nobody'd come near me, after that. Word of it even followed me into Mid-state. Added to the ear I shredded, the rap was, *Watch out for Curt, man; you pull shit with him, he'll rip your dick off by just lookin' at ya.*

When I got out of county's when I started workin' out real hard, so nobody could even sneak up an' punk me out, again. By the time I hit Mid-state, I was bulkin' up. It makes a difference, walkin' into a real prison for the first time an' bein' built like a brick shit house, as my gramma'd say. With such a major rep an' solid fists, only an idiot'd want to think about fuckin' with you, like that fuckin' Nazi proved. Good thing about it was, it gave me time to figure out how the joint worked. An' time to make a couple pals by hittin' up some old buddies on the outside to send in some Tina to pass around. By the time this one brother decided to try his territorial crap on me, I had a pack to watch my back. So he did some huffin' an' struttin' but never got down to really tryin' anything. Made the rest of my time go nice an' easy.

Funny thing is, 'cause of Paco an' his buddies, when I turned a guy into my punk, he had to be cut. Circumcised. Don't matter that I don't suck his cock, that he only sucks mine. Th' second I find out he's still got a foreskin, he's on his own, an' I spread th' word he's available. Paco's head cheese made me hate even bein' around an uncut cock.

But now here were Wayne an' Lenny lettin' me know they had a good idea my cherry was long gone. So I got snarly.

"What th' fuck do you think?" I snapped. "I'm a fuckin' kid dealin' with hard-assed cons who're in for the thousandth time. You think they give a shit 'bout me or anybody? An' let's get this straight — they didn't fuckin' make me like it."

"Which proves my point," said Wayne.

"Bullshit," I snarled. "They just didn't want to."

"But you did?"

I shrugged. I was startin' to feel like I'd chatted too much, already.

"Why?" asked Lenny. When I didn't answer, he added, "How did you learn how to do it?"

I rolled my eyes. "Practice, what the fuck you think? An' makin' sure nobody'd try that shit with me, again."

"How could you possibly make sure that — ?"

"C'mon, Lenny, that part's easy. First I built myself up like this." I stood up an' spread my arms apart, lettin' 'em see how powerful I was. "Then I punked out a couple guys who'd tried to punk me. Then I found out which guys you wanna deal with instead of fuck with, an' I let 'em use my punks. An' I fed 'em some other stuff they wanted. An' then they started lettin' me choose from the fresh meat that come in. An' when I turned 'em, bit by bit — what's that phrase? Through trial an' error? — I figured out how to make 'em like it. An' once I knew, I showed those fuckers how, no matter how much they didn't want to. Some of 'em with a wife an' five kids on the outside, always talkin' 'bout how much they liked pussy an' tits. I'd lay 'em back an' I pop their legs in the air an' I shove my dick up their ass an' I'd make 'em shoot their wads while I fucked 'em on their backs, just like you fuck a woman. An' not just once; I did it to some of 'em over an' over. I made 'em like it. I made 'em think they were queer for a man's dick up their ass. I showed 'em who was boss. It wasn't so hard to do."

Wayne was lookin' at me with wide eyes, again, but he still wasn't backin' down. "That was in prison," he said, so soft I almost couldn't hear him. "It's a rarified environment, where men have few normal outlets for sex."

"So...fuckin'...what?! You think I'm lyin'? You think I couldn't drag some guy in off the street an' do it to him, right now?!"

Lenny got up an' put his hand on my arm, saying, "Curt, why don't you sit back down? Let me get you a nice cold beer."

That's when I realized I was standin' over Wayne an' he was frozen against the corner of the couch, lookin' like he thought I was gonna pop him. An' maybe I was about to. So I took in a deep breath, let Lenny have my bottle, stepped back an' flexed to let off some of the tension in my back, then sat back on the chair. Lenny headed into the kitchen. His eyes never left me.

Wayne was tryin' real hard to sound cool when he asked, "So you got guys to cum just by fucking them?"

I shrugged. I could of told him there was more to it than that, but all of a sudden I wasn't in a sharin' kind of mood.

Lenny came back in with an ice cold one, cast a hard look at Wayne an' said, "Then he was probably massaging their prostate. That can force a man into an erection, and even an ejaculation. Which must mean you have a huge dick."

I could tell from how his hand shook that it was playtime. I'd spooked 'em an' they wanted to get me done an' gone before I got too much drunker. So what the fuck; get it over with. Why not?

"Almost ten inches," I said.

"No," was all Lenny could say.

I chuckled an' said, "I can prove it."

Lenny was back to all but dancin'. He'd already put my snarl from a minute ago straight out of his head. "You mean, I could measure it? See for myself?"

I slid deeper into the chair, stretchin' an' lettin' my body do its job. Wayne was lookin' me over with a wary interest that added to the warnin' bells in my brain. Now it was me ready to end it.

"Tell you what," I said. "Let's bet on it. Two hundred says I am. A freebie, if I'm not."

Lenny hesitated. Wayne didn't move. Lenny looked at him an' asked, "What do you think?"

Wayne licked his lips...an' I knew I had him, even for all the crap he'd shot at me. "For both of us?" he asked.

I smiled an' said, "Two-fifty."

Lenny went to a desk an' pulled out a ruler. Wayne pulled a hundred, a fifty an' five twenties from his wallet. I couldn't believe it; the dumb fuck's smart enough to know carryin' that much around with him is askin' for trouble. He put it on the table.

I stood up, stretched, again, an' slid my zipper down, real slow. Makin' 'em wait was half the fun. Then I pulled my dick out. They both looked at it like they'd never seen one, before.

I started playin' with it to get it hard, but Lenny jumped over to stop me. "I want to check something out," he said, then he took my dick an' lay it on the ruler an' whispered, "Five and a half inches, soft. Now let me." An' he began strokin' me. Wayne got closer, to watch. I just stood there.

It didn't take long to get me hard; Lenny had good strong hands. An' Wayne finally helped him by slippin' my balls out an' rollin' 'em with his fingers. Through it all, I closed my eyes an' thought about nothin'. I never did think when I was lettin' a guy do me. My mind'd just go blank, like I was in a trance, even though I knew I wasn't. It's weird how it happens. Anyway, when I was as big as I could get, Lenny put the ruler alongside my dick an' whistled. "Nine and three-quarters," he said. "Close enough," an' then he slipped his mouth around me.

It wasn't the best blowjob I ever got, but it wasn't the worst, either. An' Wayne joined him. They kept swappin' mouths between my dick an' my balls, an' it felt good like that, so I let 'em put their hands wherever they wanted. So long as they didn't pull my jeans down any lower. An' as I was close to takin' off, I started thinkin', *That'll show you, Connie. Fuckin' cunt. I'm the one in control, here.*

When I was done, I felt — I dunno, I can't really describe

it. I felt...easy. Full. Relaxed. Wanted. All of it. An' I noticed Lenny an' Wayne'd taken care of themselves at the same time — one hand for each other, one for me. Wayne was still jugglin' my balls an' strokin' my dick an' I didn't want him to stop. Even when he ran his hands up the insides of my legs an' around an' up over my butt. I liked the feelin's it brought, weird ones that were comfortable. Casual. Calm. But I couldn't let him think that that's what I liked, so that's when I took the money off the table an' shoved it in my pocket. Then I tucked my dick away.

Lenny lay back against the couch, smilin' like a cat that just ate some dumb bird. Wayne was still runnin' his hands over me. Now he was behind me, runnin' his hands under my arms an' over my pecs like he was worshipin' me, or somethin'. Then he started gettin' lower, goin' back down around my butt, again, so I stepped away from him an' drank down the last of my beer.

"I better split," I said.

"You don't have to," said Wayne.

I shrugged an' set the bottle on the table. "Naw, I got a ways to go to get home."

"Long drive?" asked Lenny.

"Walk," I said. "I got no car."

"We could drive you," said Wayne.

"Don't want you to."

I headed for the door.

"You want a car?" asked Lenny.

I stopped an' looked at him, thinkin' I knew what he meant. A little more serious *fun time* an' I'd get a set of wheels. An' to be honest, I was up for it — dependin' on what he was wantin' in the way of *fun time*. "Why, you got one you don't need?"

Lenny didn't move, just let his eyes drift in my direction as he said, "Yes. A Chevy. Not a new one, but it runs good."

"What's it gonna cost?"

"You show me how you did it."

I didn't get it. Neither did Wayne — or I don't think he did. I was pretty much ready to think I didn't know anything about how Wayne thought. He looked at Lenny like he was talkin' some weird language an' said, "You want him to come back?"

"Yes," said Lenny. "Then I want him to show me how he did it. Prove he did it."

"Did what?" I asked.

"Made 'em cum."

Now I'm not gonna tell ya I really thought about what Lenny was sayin'. I didn't. Didn't even really think about what it meant. Didn't wonder why he wanted to know. Didn't consider it'd be messin' with a guy in the community who'd never done a thing to me instead of with a con who was kicked into my path by those self-righteous assholes that run the country. I didn't tell myself I wasn't queer or that I oughta be doin' a girl instead of a guy, even tho' I'd never even thought about doin' anything like that to any chick since I had Connie to fuck with. Or that what Lenny was askin' me to do was worth prison, an' that if I was caught it'd be my second strike. I didn't even get pissed at his real meanin' — that he thought I was full of shit an' couldn't back up what I'd said. All I thought was, "You'll give me a car?"

"An eighty-seven Malibu," said Lenny. "My father's car. Low mileage. Runs good. He died a year ago an' I just haven't gotten around to selling it. I'll sign it over to you if you'll show me how you did it. And let me videotape it all."

Tape me?! Now that made me stop an' think. It got Wayne goin', too.

"Lenny, are you out of your fucking mind?" he sniped. "Do you have any idea how fucking illegal that is?"

"Only if you get caught," Lenny said, right back him. "But if we play our cards right, we won't."

That brought a big *huh?* from me. "What d'ya mean? It's one thing to do a guy in prison; the uniforms don't give a fuck what happens to any of us. Or in some back-assed state like Texas, where it's open season on fags. But grab a guy off the street in the community? In L-A? He's gonna call th' cops."

"Curt's right, Lenny. It's better to leave that idea in fantasy land."

"But what if he's someone who wouldn't go to the police?"

Lenny asked. "What if, once it's done, we give him a lot of money and he chalks the experience up to being part of his business?"

Wayne sat on the sofa's arm an' talked to Lenny like he was a kid that just got caught smokin'. "If you mean doing that to one of the boys down on Santa Monica, some night — come on, they aren't exactly what you'd call straight. And God only knows what sorts of diseases they carry — AIDS, syphilis, herpes, you name it, they probably have it and have done it."

"I know, Wayne. Will you at least try to give me some credit, for once? I'm talking about hiring an escort."

"Which raises the same issue about whether or not they're straight!"

"Doesn't matter. Most of those guys swear they're hetero. But even if he isn't, if we hire him from one of those ads and we...well, hold him down and let Curt do his thing, it'd be a pretty damn good facsimile. And that's all I really care about — watching him do it to someone who doesn't want to do it. And making him like it. All on tape."

Wayne stood up, lookin' kind of weird. "I can't believe you're suggesting such a thing."

"I can't fuckin' believe you wanna tape it," I chimed in, an' not too happily, I'd say. But Lenny didn't notice.

"It's just for me, Curt," he said. "A one-time experiment to prove your point. Videotaped so I can look at it as many times as I want and — " He gave the international motion for jackin' off.

"You're fuckin' sick," I snarled.

Lenny looked at me, point blank, an' got this expression on his face that...I dunno...seemed simple an' natural an' scary all at the same time. "No, Curt," he said in a plain voice, "I'm fucking old. And I'm fucking tired. And the only way I *can* fuck, anymore, is to pay for it. As we saw, tonight, an' that isn't even what I'd really call fucking. And I'm so fucking weary of that. And I'm so fucking close to being broke because of it."

"Lenny," Wayne started, but he got cut off with a look.

"If you don't want to be part of it, Wayne, don't be. Tell you what, you go home to Kansas for a week, and we'll do it then. You go back to a state where it's okay to send queers to jail for making love, no matter what the Supreme Court says, and that happily tolerates a motherfucker who tells people to kill us. Go back to a place where the only way you can make contact with something male is to pick up a guy in the park who'll only let you suck his dick, and then who'll beat you up and take your money, knowing you won't be able to go to the cops about it. Go back and try to remember why the hell you ran like crazy to get away from that kind of world. And why I did."

He clenched his teeth then looked back at me. "Curt, most of my sexual contact now comes from my right hand. If that's how the rest of my life's going to be, fine. But I want something to make it worthwhile. And if that means messing with somebody who's been messing with guys like me...even better. Now I'm offering you a car that's in good running order. One that's worth thousands of dollars. And all I want you to do is give me a little something back. You don't really have to rape a nice straight heterosexual male; one of the fake ones will do. But I want to watch you do it. I want to watch you make one of those obnoxious pretty-boy fucks who've taken my money over and over and over into your bitch and love it, so I can withdraw into my own little world and fantasize about doing it, myself."

"Fantasize?" I asked, believin' his bullshit about as much as I believed in the tooth fairy.

"Of course," he said. "Do I look like someone who could do something like that, himself. Not really. All I could ever do is jack off."

He stood up an' looked at me, face t' face. An' I knew he was right. He was weak. Nervous. Bitin' the nail of his thumb, he was so freaked out at even the thought of what he'd just suggested. He'd be way too much of a pussy to ever really try it on his own. Too scared everything'd go wrong and he'd wind up in jail. He needed somebody to do it for him, an' he was willin' to pay for the pleasure of watchin' it.

An' me? What was I thinkin'? Well...fact of the matter is, I wasn't. But I still wasn't so sure about sayin' okay, just yet. I guess he thought I was about to say, *No*, so he sat on an arm of the couch, tryin' to look all sweet an innocent.

"Tell you what," he said, "I'll make you a bet. You do it and you get him off, the car's yours. Along with a thousand dollars. You don't, you give me a full-scale freebie. Anything I want for one night. I'll use that as my substitute fantasy."

He was grinnin' in this sort of bad-little-boy way, then. An' fuck me if it didn't make me grin right back at him.

"On one condition," I said before I even realized I said it. Then I saw from the corner of my eye that Wayne was lookin' at me like I was sicker than Lenny, an' that made me smirkier.

"What's that?" Lenny asked.

"There was a guy, my last year of high school, he's the one got me sent to jail. If your boy could look like him, it'd give me a fantasy, too."

"Revenge by proxy. I love it. What are the specifics?"

"You mean, what's he look like? Sort of Italian. Long face. Taller'n me. Not as built up but solid. He played baseball. Short dark hair. That'd be close enough. Oh, an' one more thing."

"What's that?"

"He's gotta be cut. His dick, I mean."

"Circumcised?" said Lenny. "No problem with that."

Wayne was all up an' down about it. "Lenny! Curt! Will you stop a minute and think! You're not just talking about you two! There'll be another person involved! What'll this do to him? Have you considered that?"

"Considered what a bit more sex than they planned on is going to do to a whore?" Lenny shot back. "Who'll be paid for the extra trouble? Who wouldn't hesitate for a second to rip us off or use us to get more money? As you know has happened." Which gave me more of a clue as to why Lenny really wanted to do it. Then he turned to me, shakin' a little, an' said, "Do you have any problem with that?"

Still not thinkin', I took a deep breath an' shook my head

an' shook his hand an' said, "Fuck, no. Set it up."

Then I gave him my phone number an' headed home.

Chapter Three

It's funny, but after agreein' to that bet, somethin' in me shifted. I didn't really notice it, at first; it's like it happened way down deep an' took its time workin' its way up to my brain. But lookin' back, I can see how, when I walked home, I looked at everything different.

An' yeah, I walked all the way back to fuckin' Hollywood. I will not in any way, form or fashion ride the fuckin' bus. Fuckin' ass-wipes who run the Metro system but ride to work in limos, they let the fuckin' things get to where they're disgustin'. Old skanky busses that break down more than they work. Spittin' exhaust in through a two-bit a/c that ain't good enough for a fuckin' Honda. Seats covered with gum an' spit an' ink an' God knows what else. Dozens of smelly little third-worlders sittin' side by side or standin' forty deep an' chatterin' in some bastard-style Mexican crap, or big black bucks handin' out attitude to anybody they fuckin' feel like 'cause they got no other way to be anybody. Me in with all them people yellin' an' fightin' an' all that shit? In a sardine can on wheels? Fuck, I knew real quick I'd kill somebody if I had to ride one of them fuckin' things every day. So I did shanks mare to my jobs an' anywhere else I had to go. Helped me blow off steam an' kept me from gettin' too close to any assholes.

So that night, as I'm walkin' home from Lenny's — feelin' really good from the blow job an' the two-fifty in my pocket an' the buzz from the beers an' even the bet — I dunno why, but it was like I'd never walked down Santa Monica before. All the buildin's were new. All the lights were bright an' cheerful. All the traffic was steady an' fun to watch. I saw this tiny little park at the corner of Crescent Heights an' wondered when the hell they put that in. I passed under street lights with big bright globes on 'em an' thought, *Ain't that neat?* I saw how many trees lined the sidewalks an' occasional islands in the middle of the road, all for the first time.

My whole attitude about Santa Monica changed. I always thought it was kind of a second-class street, the kind I'd always wind up goin' down. Not like Wilshire. Wilshire, no matter where you are on it, it's got class. It's got attitude. Style, even. But Santa Monica always seemed to be — I dunno, sayin' it was sorry for bein' so full of potholes an' for havin' such narrow sidewalks an' for bein' so old an' out of touch. Even when it passed through west West Hollywood, where it was spilt in half by trees, an' when it cut through B-Hills an' had a park on one side, it still felt sorry. Still felt like it was back alley. But not no more. Now it wasn't a crowded street in a too-big city full of five million languages; now it was a huntin' ground, an' I was a lion on the prowl.

An' the guys I'd pass? They were nothin' but my dinner. I'd smile at 'em, laughin' inside as I thought, *He don't know what I'm gonna do. What if I did it to him? Is he anybody I'd do it to? Or him?* Didn't matter if they looked good or young or queer or anything, I had this new standard for smilin' at my fellow man — was he worth prison?

So that's why I put those restrictions on Lenny-boy. If I'm gonna risk a second strike, I want it to be somethin' I'll at least enjoy. An' man, I have to admit, fuckin' up some squeaky-clean asswipe of a guy, especially if he looked a little like fuckin' Anthony, made me happy.

Now I ain't gonna tell you I was thinkin' 'bout gettin' caught. I wasn't. Thought never entered my head. I mean, come on — what *heterosexual male whore* in his right mind'll admit to bein' butt-fucked by an ex-con an' forced to cum? Think about it. Just the fact that he shot his load would make any cop or D-A really wonder if the guy was legit or if he just got into something over his head an' was freaked 'cause his family might find out an' dump him. An' if the guys at his day job found out? They'd make his life hell. He might even get fired. Not for bein' queer; oh, no, that's illegal in California. But suddenly his job ratings'd fall off an' he'd get all these black marks an' just have to be let go *for poor performance* or some bullshit like that.

I mean, everybody knows it's still okay to hate faggots in this country. Hell, in most of the world. Just listen to any so-called *man of God* go on 'bout it on Sunday mornin'. An' look at all those two-faced cocksuckers who'll tell you queers can change an' they got proof when any fuckin' idiot can see they're lyin' through their teeth and'd drop an' suck a cock the first second one was waved in their face. But hey, it's all in the name of God, so that makes hate an' stupidity an' general pissiness okay, right?

Fuckin' asswipes. They preach love an' understandin', but you take one fuckin' step that's wrong an' you're marked for life in their eyes. You want any help from 'em? You gotta be what they want you to be. You gotta change into what they think is right. You gotta live how they tell you to fuckin' live. An' if you don't? Just try an' get 'em to turn one fuckin' hand for you. *I may be a Christian, but I do not believe it when Jesus tells me to love my neighbor as myself.*

Yeah, I know the Bible. Some of it. That fuckin' priest that'd come by County thought he was gonna make me into one of his boys. Not like that, but as *a soldier in God's army*, was how he put it. We'd sit together in his office twice a week, chattin' about life an' the meanin' of God an' how I got so off track an' all that shit. He'd quote verses an' tell me where they were in the Bible. He even gave me a small one so I could look 'em up. An' I *did* start lookin' through it, more an' more, tryin' to figure out what the hell'd gone wrong with my life. Wonderin' if maybe there was an answer in those tremblin' little pages.

Now I gotta be honest — I was goin' there at first 'cause it gave me a breather from dealin' with all the shit you got in jail. Even a dinky assed county joint. Dumbshits tryin' to prove who's got th' biggest cock on a twenty-four-seven basis. Takin' letters an' pictures an' socks from guys that're weaker than them. I mean, it's pathetic, rippin' off somebody's fuckin' toothpaste to prove you're a man. Some guys had cigs stashed away, or bottles of whiskey or bits of chemicals, an' they'd swap 'em for protection. Or drugs. An' sometimes a bunch of the *big dick* boys'd gang up on a new kid, wrap him in a blanket an' fuck him, like hidin' him made it more like they were fuckin' a girl. Stupid. An' me, I was sick of it. Sick of fightin' the little fucks off all the time when they wanted my shit, even after Paco. Sick of gettin' into noise-fights over if I gave one of 'em a dirty look or not. Sick of always havin' to watch my back in case some *big dick* who didn't believe the shit spread about me decided he wanted to make me back into his new mouth. That's why I never missed Father Tello's little meetin's.

He was all about readin' the Gospels an' followin' in the teachin's of Christ an' all that. So that's what I read. An' what's really funny is, for about ten minutes I sort of believed in it. Matthew, verses five through seven. *Sermon on the Mount*, he called it. All the stuff about not judgin' others an' lovin' thy neighbor an' doin' unto others like you want them to do to you. An' I'm thinkin', *Shit, I wish I'd been told about this shit.* It was somethin' to live by, a guidebook for a kid who was tryin' to figure life out on his own an' doin' a pretty fucked up job of it.

Y'see, my mom...well, let's face it — she was a slut who'd do anything for a drink, though she'd never admit to that now. She's all married an' respectable an' born-again into the middle class with two daughters that're honest kids, not fatherless bastards like me an' my brother. She really said that to me, once, leadin' up to tellin' me how I'm the bastard she didn't want to have. But since she lived in this dinky-assed town in Wyoming an' the guy who usually did her abortions'd been slammed into jail an' the nearest legal clinic was in fuckin' Denver, I got born. Considerin' how I turned out, she felt it was too bad she couldn't make it to Denver.

Y'know, we spent more'n six years in that stinkin' hell-hole of a Wyoming town. With my mom turnin' tricks at the truck stop for money for booze. An' her mom makin' sure I got fed an' my diapers got changed an' I got a hug, once in a while, an' all that shit. At least, till she keeled over from a heart attack that nobody — not the paramedics or the E-R doctors — believed was a heart attack till it killed her. I was four. By the time I hit six, I'd figured out how to fix my own cereal an' rip off milk from other doorsteps an' keep myself goin' while mom slept off her drunks.

We didn't move to LA till the state tried to take me away from her. Fuckin' bureaucrats an' *Christian* folk didn't give a shit about me till my grandmother was dead from takin' care of me an' my mom got preggers, again. Then, by God, they wanted to make fuckin' sure I was raised right. Same for the kid my mom was carryin'. Fuckin' hypocrites. They didn't give a fuck about my mom gettin' abortions till her usual guy cut too deep into some rich bitch's scared little girl an' she bled to death; then they ended the *illegal* practice everybody in town knew about. Those *good Christian folk* who turned my mom in, they wouldn't take me in or any kid like me. No fuckin' way. That'd mean practicin' what they preached, an' that might be real inconvenient. No, I was gonna get farmed out to some foster family who were more interested in the state stipend than in me, an' if that didn't work then I'd get dumped onto the state. So me an' mom, we split in th' middle of the night with some trucker who just loved her mouth.

Jesus, over the next seven years we lived in every part of Southern California there was. LA. Oxnard. Oceanside — mom loved Marines for some fuckin' reason; maybe my dad was one, once. Riverside — which stinks, an' I mean really. San Bernadino. Santa Clarita. Palmdale. Ojai. You name it, I could probably give you an address there. An' she turned tricks the whole time. Till she married this insurance salesman from Pasadena who *didn't care about her past.* By that point, I was thirteen goin' on thirty, an' nobody had say over me but me. Still, things calmed down a lot. For a while. Till I realized he was a cheap-assed son-of-a-bitch who only took my brother an' me in 'cause we came with the package an' he wasn't gonna give either of us a fuckin' penny more'n he had to. An' I got goin' in the drug biz. An' wound up at county.

Anyhow, when I was eighteen, I got dumped me out on the world. I couldn't go home if I'd wanted to. My mom an' her motherfucker told me there was no fuckin' way they'd let me back in; I was too *out of control* and'd be a *bad influence on the other kids*. An' I had nobody else to hold onto. All I had was a few bucks an' the address for a halfway house in Silver Lake. So I headed there. Tello's church was in Hollywood. I figured he'd help me get a job an' get my life goin' right.

But he didn't do shit. Didn't make one fuckin' call. Didn't return calls when I gave him as a reference. Got to where he was always *in a meetin'* when I tried t' call him. It's like I didn't exist, anymore. For a while, I thought I'd done somethin' t' piss him off, but I couldn't figure out what. I mean, I was workin' a regular job at a burger joint for slave wage. I was stayin' in the halfway house. I'd stopped doin' drugs, complete. It didn't' make sense. Then this kid named Mario who was in county before me explained it.

"Out of sight, out of mind," he said. I didn't get it, at first, so Mario laid out the full 4-1-1. "You ain't around him, no more, vato. He's like this lifeguard that says he'll save ya from drownin' but when ya really need him, he's on his lunch break an' it's your own damn fault for tryin' to drown at that time. He thinks he did all he had to do while you was inside. Now it's up to you to make it. Even if you drown."

God, I felt like a dumb fuck.

But I ain't one, now. I'm not *educated*. My grammar sucks an' my two-plus-two's are about as basic as you can get. But I ain't stupid, not no more. I know how to take stuff that I need an' not get caught. I know how to get what I can't take without bein' caught. I can do whatever I got to do to keep myself goin' an' not worry 'bout it till it's done, if then. I guess you'd call that bein' an animal, but if you're treated like a dog, that's what you get to be. Like a dog.

A dog.

Shit. That reminds me of this cousin of my mom's, lived in Montana. Butte, maybe. He was a mean-assed SOB who wouldn't do jack for anybody, not even his own family. An' he had a dog. A scared little mutt he treated like shit. Kicked it. Barely fed it. Yelled at it. I saw him do all that shit the one time I was there. How old was I? Five? Maybe six. Maybe just before we left. Yeah, I think mom went to him for money an' he whined about how broke he was or somethin'. Had a brand new Ford truck, I noticed, but he still whined about not havin' any money. Asshole.

Anyway, I saw that dog gettin' knocked around by one of his kids — this nasty little fuck named George — an' it bit him. I laughed when I saw it; I mean, the little fuck deserved it. But when his asshole father found out what happened, he pulled out a pistol an' shot the dog as it cowered in a corner. Then after he dropped us off at the bus station the next mornin', he went off to get another one.

I asked my mom why he'd be allowed to do that, an' she snapped, "What the fuck do you care? We got our own shit to worry about."

I used to have nightmares about that dog. Till I finally caught on to what my mom was talkin' about an' started actin' on it. Right about the time my mom decided she wanted to change her life. Too late for that, for me, though. But then I met Connie, an' she's the one who brought me back to humanity. For a little while, anyway.

I met her at this rave downtown. I was the promoter's main connection for X — ecstasy for those who ain't payin' attention — an' I was sellin' off some extra tabs for a nice little profit in the mosh pit. I never did that crap, myself; it was too much fun watchin' all the neon glow sticks an' pacifiers swirlin' in the darkness. Lots of slim sweaty boys an' slick hot girls twistin' 'round an' glidin' into each other while some overpaid DJ dropped tunes. That promoter was a cheap bastard; he never had live bands. Besides, if I *had* gotten wasted it would've been way too easy to get into the rhythm of the night, an' I'd probably have wound up givin' the crap away to keep the joy goin'. An' I might've missed seein' her. Seein' Connie standin' stock still in the middle of all those fuckin' gorgeous guys an' girls. No glow stick. No pacifier. Just a bottle of water an' little smile on her face as she watched 'em dance. God, she looked hot.

I swung over to her, but she saw me comin' an' raised a finger at me. "Not for me, buddy; I gotta work, tomorrow."

"Wasn't gonna offer," I said — even though I really was, as a way of gettin' t' talk with her. "Just wanted to ask you to dance."

She looked at me, real tight. "You're straight."

"In every way."

"I meant you're not flying."

"An' I meant in every way."

She looked me over an' nodded. I ain't gonna be fake an' modest, here; I knew I looked good. I wasn't as built up as I am now, but I was done up okay. An' I could see from her eyes she saw me as a one-nighter, someone over for a quickie. Which was fine with me.

So we danced an' did the bullshit thing. She was workin' on a cheap-assed indie flick in Venice, some soft-porn thing for the European video market. I got the hint that she'd watched some of the shootin' an' got horny from it. I told her I was open to doin' somethin' like that. She told me the pay sucked. I told her I was workin' at bein' a contractor, do roofin' repair an' shit. Which was bull an' she knew it, but she didn't give a fuck. She took me home to her place an' we found out just how perfect we were for each other, that night. Holy shit, did we find out. She had to go to work with maybe two hours sleep, but she went purrin', lemme tell ya.

I moved in with her two weeks later, an' we got married two months after that. An' for three years, it was cool. Shit, it was perfect. She got herself out of the soft-porn crap an' into some pretty damn good indie flicks. "Things that're being made by the mini-majors," as she put it. An' me, I got into the paintin' gig, doin' houses an' small buildin's an' workin' on sets when Connie referred me. An' we fucked every night an' loved it. Loved it till I got busted for doin' a buddy a favor.

Guy named Terrence, who asked me to cart a couple bags of coke to a friend of his. I'd done it before, so I figured no big deal. Only Terrence'd been busted an' was workin' the cops to cut down on his time inside, an' he was turnin' over anybody an' everybody he'd ever worked with, me included. So I got grabbed with two kilos of coke in my backpack an' was handed a sentence of eight to twenty for possession with intent to distribute. The asshole. I made sure word got into his mini-security facility that he was a skunk. I hear his time inside was made wonderful by those who could do it to him, anytime.

Shit, fuckin' Terrence. There's another asswipe I'd like to take care of. Not like I was gonna do with this bet; that fuck was too fuckin' skanky for me to even think about it.

An' don't start thinkin' I'm a racist. Me not wantin' to fuck Terrence's got nothin' to do with his color; it's got to do with the fact that he's an ugly fuck an' had some kind of prejudice against bathin' more'n once a year. I don't care what race a guy is, so long as he looks decent an' keeps himself clean. An' such.

I mean, I once wondered what it'd be like to do my thing with Will Smith, if he wound up inside. He looked like he'd be fun an' frisky. Not that I'd even really thought of tryin' t' connect with him on the outside — I'm not queer for man-sex, don't y'know — but he's one of the few black guys I've seen who's not just black, if that makes sense. I mean, he's just a guy, y'know? A good-lookin' guy, an' I'm comfortable 'round them for some weird reason. Good-lookin' girls I just wanna fuck. Good-lookin' guys, I wanna be pals. Wanna be buds. Tight buds, y'know?

Even fuckin' Anthony, as much as I hate the fucker, I — shit, I gotta admit, I *did* want to be buds with him. He wasn't the Big Man On Campus; the football quarterback always got that job 'cause, for some weird reason every one of 'em looked like they should've been on a box of *Wheaties*. But Anthony, as uptight an' *proper* as he was, he played ball like it oughta be played — easy an' natural, like he was destined for the majors. He actually made it to the big leagues for a few years, till he ruined his knee slidin' into home, one game. I think that's why I let him con me into givin' him that joint — for a buck, which didn't even cover its cost; that an' I sort of wanted to see just how loose he'd get once he got stoned.

Y'see, he reminded me of pictures I saw of the guy mom said was my old man. Some hippie or yippie or whatever they were called at that time, passin' through Wyomin' on his way to Seattle. In a VW Microbus that wouldn't go more'n sixty downhill. He picked my mom up in Cheyenne an' she rode with him up to Sheridan — that was mom's moneymaker route — an' somewhere along in there I got started.

"For free," she said, "'cause he looked like Jesus."

An' he did. It's weird. She took some Polaroids of him by a creek in the middle of nowhere an' he seemed to glow in 'em. Long brown hair. Deep sleepy eyes...he was probably stoned. Golden skin. An expression of peace an' happiness...no, he was definitely stoned. Even with somethin' of a beard, you could tell he had a strong chin an' good nose — like mine. An' he had a perfect mouth. A man's mouth; I got more my mom's lips. He was wearin' this Indian-lookin' pullover that was so light, you could almost see through it, an' that with tight low-cut jeans, you could tell he was in good shape. I got some good genes off him. Wonder what ever happened to him, 'cause she never saw him, again. Never heard from him. Nothin'. He probably don't even know he's got me as a son. Lucky fuck. Who'd want t' be related to a guy who's dumb-fuck enough to get sent to jail by some tight-assed dumbfuck he's tryin' t' be friends with for buck's worth of pot?

Shit, where was I? Walkin' down Santa Monica. Smilin' at the faggots who looked me over an' whistled an' made their faggoty little comments an' shit. An' the whole way I'm thinkin', *Dream about it, cocksuckers. I don't need you, right now. I'm in control, asswipes. I'm king of the fuckin' world.*

I didn't realize it, then, but lookin' back I can see that's when I first got this hint of an idea of what it was I really needed. Control. Power. No matter what you call it, makin' another guy do what you want him to do when he'd never want to do it on his own — that's the best feelin' in the world as regards bein' the man. I felt it with my first punk, when somethin' behind my heart started racin'. Somethin' deep inside me that said, *Fuck drugs, fuck booze, fuck worries forever. Right now, you are the master. You ARE in control. You ARE the man, an' you ain't nobody who can get pissed on.* An' here I was about to get it, again.

I dunno if I can really get across the feelin's I caught hold of as I walked down that street. The tingle of my jeans an' shirt not...not rubbin' but whisperin' against my thighs an' pecs an' tits an' ass, makin' me feel like I could cum without a thought. The cool night air movin' round my face. The breezes whipped up as busses an' cars zipped past me in the opposite direction. The sounds of silence over long stretches of the street, where the cars an' trucks an' busses were stopped at one corner or another. It all added to the moment. I was startin' to feel...I dunno, light headed, I guess.

I passed the *pink* part of Santa Monica an' headed into the *red-light* area. Passed tired lookin' kids waitin' by bus stops in hopes of makin' fifty bucks for the night. Most of 'em looked like the junked-out tossed-aside runaways that they were an' it almost hurt to see 'em. But some of 'em were still kinda fresh. Kinda still with an attitude. An' as I passed 'em an' they glanced me over to see if I was gonna be their next John, I'd think, *I could take you back into an alley an' make you give me what you charge for, no problem.* An' it'd give me a jolt that shot from behind my heart an' into my balls an' spread over my thighs to make me even crazier.

Then I passed Highland an' zigged up to Sunset, since my crib was up near Franklin an' Cahuenga. That brought me past the *A Club*, an' I saw these sleek neat *Young Hollywood* guys in their clean pressed shirts an' hundred dollar jeans bouncin' in an' out of the place, all tryin' to look hot for these tiny Hollywood sluts with inflatable tits who had zero interest in 'em unless they had cash enough to buy 'em more than a leaf of lettuce to eat. I stopped across the little side street an' watched a group of guys by the entrance, laughin' an' clappin' each other on th' back an' actin' like a bunch of frat boys an' I thought, *I could wipe those smiles off your faces, punks, one right after the other. Punk you out, one after the other. All in one night. All together. An' I'd have the time of my life doin' it.*

Then one of 'em headed right for me. A big blond buck with perfect teeth an' perfect hair an' still perfect shirt, even after hours of playin' pool an' downin' beers. He looked like he probably played football in college. Tight end or half-back or somethin' that called for speed an' agility. But he wasn't keepin' himself up. He still had broad shoulders but they couldn't hide the gut he was startin' to get. But he was wearin' these black jeans that made his ass look inviting. An' when he turned away from me an' headed up the side street, I followed him.

I dunno why I did, I have to admit. Nothin' hit me in th' form of a thought as to what I was gonna do. I just saw how happy he looked, an' how easy his life'd been an' how perfect it would be from then on. So I followed him. Watched him jaunt towards this three year old Dodge parked halfway between two street lights. Watched his ass move under those jeans. Even th' way he walked screamed at me how happy he was...

An' I knew I had to kill that walk.

I dug in my pockets for somethin', anythin' I could use for a weapon to make him come with me. Shit, all I had was a fingernail clipper. But it had a file, an' the file was sharp. If I held it right, he'd never know. I mean, if a guy believes you can cut him, you don't really have to be able to, right?

He *beeped* off his alarm an' got to his car an' opened his door an' I was about to make my move when I heard, "Hey, Chad!" behind me. I went cold, but I didn't stop. Didn't even hesitate. Just kept walkin' right by him as I heard somebody run up to him an' chatter loudly, "I'm comin' with you. Rob's got too much shit in his back seat."

"Fuckin' dick," I heard Chad say. "What you wanna bet his crib's the same way?"

"If it is, I'm gone."

I heard two car doors slam an' th' car roar to life as I kept headin' down the street. A second later, they zoomed past me, radio blarin' with some second-rate rocker's rendition of *Relax* an' turned left to go back to Sunset.

An' I dropped to my knees.

I mean, I was shakin' like you wouldn't believe. Like I was scared. But I wasn't scared, that's what's so freaky about it. I was pissed off that he got away. *Really* fuckin' pissed. I wanted to chase that fuckin' Dodge down the street an' fuck Chad's fuckin' buddy, Rob, in the ass an' in th' mouth an' rip his fuckin' dick off an' shove it up his ass for helpin' fuckin' Chad get away from me. I dug my nails into the sidewalk, wishin' it was fuckin' Chad's fuckin' face I was rippin' apart. I tore my fingers up, good, but it didn't help. I leaned against the wall of this ratty old buildin' an' sat there, fightin' to shut the anger down, but I couldn't. I could feel myself drownin' in it, even as I wondered where the hell it came from.

I don't remember standin' up, but suddenly I was half-walkin'-half-stumblin' back to Sunset. I don't remember seein' a clock, but somehow I knew it was after one. I heard music — I remember it bein' like dance. Like what I'd hear at the raves I went to. But I don't know what the song was or anything; it just fed the mess in my brain. I remember there was a bar down the street, some kind of club with a long line of people waitin' to get in. An' people laughin' an' chatterin' while they waited. Couples. Good-lookin' couples, like there used to be. Fuckin' happy good-lookin' couples. Shit, that fed the mess, too. I wanted t' head on. Go home t' Connie. But I felt sick. My stomach was churnin' an' it was all I could do to lean back against that buildin' right at the corner of th' side street an' try to keep from hurlin'.

Is that how a lion feels when he loses his kill? Is that why they roar an' pace an' snarl after they've got themselves all primed up for a feast an' then find their fresh meat's been able to skit away to safety? Not defeated. Not hungry. Just fuckin' pissed off. Am I *that* much of an animal?

My hands dropped between my legs an' I jolted. They'd brushed against my crotch an' I realized for the first time I had a major hard-on. I'd forgot I wasn't wearin' briefs. I'd got so used to them, since leavin' Mid-State. I'd never really liked boxers, except to sleep in. Always liked briefs when I'm in jeans. Felt more protected.

Oh, fuck, oh, fuck, oh, fuck, oh, fuck.

I almost couldn't breathe, I felt so raw.

It felt raw. My dick. I left my right hand down there an' I let it rock up an' down a little on it, sendin' explosions over my thighs and up my back an' into my mind. Maybe if I kept doin' that, everything'd be okay.

Oh, fuck, oh, fuck, oh, fuck, I wanted to go home to Connie. I wanted to get hold of her and not let go. I wanted to pretend this whole night'd never happened. That I never met Wayne an' Lenny. That I never went to their place an' talked about my life an' made that bet thinkin' it'd make me feel better. 'Cause it wouldn't. I could see that. I could see they helped feed this — this roar of anger in me that I'd almost lost control of. I never wanted to talk with those two little fucks, again. Never.

But nothin' was helpin'.

Nothin' was helpin'.

Knowin' that didn't mean shit. Seein' that didn't mean fuck. I still had that hard-on an' the churnin' in my gut an' the roar in my brain. An' I was startin' to drown in it. Startin' to drown. Knowin' this is crazy. This is fuckin' crazy, Curt!

Fuckin' crazy!

Then I heard somebody walkin' towards me. Heavy feet. One set. Prob'ly boots. Prob'ly a guy. I looked around an' could of sworn it was daylight, the lamps were so bright. I ducked my face down to keep it in shadow. I didn't look up till I knew he was passin' me. No thought. No nothin'. I just grabbed him from behind an' slung him against the wall an' pressed my file to his throat an' snarled, "Shh...shh, not a fuckin' word. Not a fuckin' word."

I shoved him down to this sort-of alley — my arm tight around his neck, the file diggin' into his skin — till we slammed against this dumpster. He was tryin' to say somethin', but my arm was too tight on his throat.

"Shut up," was all I could say. Could snarl, really.

Before he knew what I was doin', I'd yanked down his pants an' shoved myself inside him. He tried to yell, but it got caught in his throat, I had so good a hold on him. He couldn't even call for help. Then I did to him what I wanted to do to Curt — I mean, Chad.

Shit, it was perfect. Just bein' inside him made it all good, again. Quiet. Peaceful. I didn't take so long, this time. I got it over, quick an' dirty. An' when I was done an' the guy was lyin' on the ground, chokin' an' moanin' an' gaspin', I kicked him in the back — two, three times — an' walked away. An' when I finally got home, I woke Connie up an' fucked her, too.

Shit. Shit, that guy — t' this day, I couldn't tell you what he looked like or how old he was or even for sure that he was a guy instead of a girl. Well, that part I knew for sure 'cause of what I made him do, an' how I smeared his face with it. I just remember that when I had control of him, it felt right. Felt good. So...damn...fuckin'...good. He was mine. Even out in the middle of fuckin' Hollywood. With cars drivin' by just a few feet away an' people walkin' by just a few yards away an' cops keepin' their eyes out for homeless people to roust just a block away, an' even God watchin' from all that far away, he was mine. Nobody else's. All mine, an' I could do what I fuckin' wanted with him an' make him do what I fuckin' wanted an' he couldn't do a fuckin' thing about it. An' that's what I did.

An' Jesus Christ, I couldn't wait t' do it, again.

Chapter Four

We set it up for the next Saturday. Be there. Call our guy at six. Have him over by eight or nine. I'd take him down then the two of us'd carry him to the bedroom. I'd do my thing. Should be done by eleven. Pay him an' kick his ass out an' go scoutin' for a beer or two by midnight. An' if he gave us any trouble, Lenny had some Cat to slip him, an' let him try an' make sense after that. So we were ready. All nice an' neat an' scheduled out like a battle plan.

Lenny decided to use one of those *model/escort* characters who got ads in the back of the weekly fag-rags. I bet he spent hours lookin' 'em over, comparin' *Scott* with *Tad* an' *Midwest Stud* with *Italian Stallion* an' on an' on. Dreamin' of how it'd go. Jackin' off to it. You'd of thought he was plannin' his weddin', or somethin'. The guy he finally settled on called himself *Jeremy*.

I had to admit, *Jeremy* sounded right. *Straight stud loves to get serviced. Junior in college. 6-1, 185, 30" waist, swimmer's body, 8 by 5 1/2 an' cut* — I don't get what that means, but no way in hell did I want to ask Lenny or Wayne; sometimes you just gotta know what info you don't need to know, y'know? — *Your wet dream cum true.* Of course. No picture, but Lenny didn't care.

"He claims he's straight," Lenny said. "That makes it even more like the real thing, right?"

I snickered at it. Snickered at any guy who says he's straight but makes his livin' gettin' sucked off by another guy. Or more. *Gay for pay*, my ass. When I get sucked off, it's 'cause

I got no other way to get some quick cash. Short of dealin', again. An' deep in the back of my mind, I know I'm thinkin' of Connie the whole time. Like it's her doin' it. 'Course, that's the only way I *can* do somethin' like that with Connie. She hates suckin' on my dick. On anybody's dick. Her attitude is, Why not just fuck? So that's what we'd do. Havin' a guy suck me off was just a change of pace. An' like I said, in prison you get to learn real quick — a mouth's a mouth. But payin' to put ads in some twinky West Hollywood piece of superficial shit newspaper? An' makin' a livin' at it? What bullshit.

So I come over around four an' Lenny showed me the setup. He'd prepped the guest bedroom, downstairs, takin' out all the pictures an' furniture, leavin' only a four-poster bed an' its sheets. Rope was coiled at each corner of the bed. The walls were covered with thick black cloth to muffle any noises the guy might make, even though he'd be gagged. An' a video camera was set up in a corner on a tripod, ready to start tapin'. It looked...creepy.

I nodded to the ropes an' asked, "What's that for?"

"See how things go," said Lenny. "I might want to — oh, make use of him, myself, when you're done. In an oral manner."

I just shook my head. Then Lenny took me back in the livin' room an' showed me the camera by the front door. It was set up on a tripod behind some plants — Ficus? Rubber? I never can tell — an' it took in the whole room. You had to look hard to see it. It made me feel even creepier.

"Was that here the other night?" I asked him.

Lenny shook his head maybe a little too fast an' said, "No, of course not. Don't you remember how dark it was? Not enough light to shoot by."

I didn't really believe him, but I wasn't gonna screw things up by bein' a dick about it. Not now. I could always find out later.

Then Lenny showed me a pair of handcuffs he'd bought at some leather shop. They weren't the best lookin' pair I'd ever seen; fact is, I figure he got ripped off on 'em. They wouldn't hold nobody who didn't want to be held. Not for long, anyways. Didn't matter; I wasn't plannin' on usin' handcuffs, anyway.

"What're you going to use?" he asked, after I told him.

"These." I showed him some thick plastic strips with a tiny loop on one end. The dykes I worked for used 'em to tie their oversized trash bags an' cops used somethin' like 'em, now, instead of handcuffs. "They work lots better."

He nodded, just like a monkey in heat. Freak.

Through all of this, Wayne'd only shown his head once, at the top of the stairs. An' that was just to shake it at us, in disgust, an' say, "This isn't right."

"Go back to your room, Wayne," said Lenny, "and maybe I'll let you watch the video once we're done. Unless you'd care to join us once everything's — oh, underway? I have the rope ready."

"Don't be disgusting," he snapped back as he glared at me. "You're going to jail, you know. And I'll laugh at you the whole time you're in."

Man, talk about a pathetic line; Wayne was so full of shit with his *holier than thou* garbage. If somebody don't want you to do something wrong, they stop you. Plain an' simple. They don't watch you make your plans to call up some guy an' bullshit him into comin' over to make a couple hundred just so you can get hold of him an' then just say, *But it's not right.* Fuck that. Deep down, he wanted to do it as much as Lenny did; he just didn't have the balls to admit it. So he's givin' himself this weaselly little out, where he can honestly say, *I told 'em not to.* An' since it ain't a crime to prevent a crime or report one in California, he could probably of got off.

So I looked straight at him an' told him flat out, "It don't matter if you get the fuck out or you stay in your room, somethin' goes wrong I'll tell people you was in with us all the way, t'night."

That way, if he pulled anything, if he told anybody, he'd go inside, too. Then I'd make damn sure his balls got cut off an' jammed up his ass by some big stinkin' uncut Nazi fucker. That shut him the fuck up...but he gave me that look, the one that creeped me all over. I eyed him, right back; neither one of us said anything, but I had the bells ringin' in my brain, again. I think he saw my face grabbin' a wary look, so he just sneered an' disappeared back up the stairs.

Fuckin' Wayne. What the fuck was he up to? Were both these cameras really connected to his bedroom TV so he could watch? Was he gonna direct this thing from his little *safe* room like you do some TV game show? *Fuck the boy for a prize?* Or was he plannin' somethin' even hinkier? I couldn't tell, an' that made me worry.

But then I noticed it was six an' Lenny was callin' the guy up to get his details. Short dark hair — good. Blue eyes — don't remember what color Anthony's were. Frat boy — right look. Lifts weights, but not too much 'cause he don't want his muscles to get too tight — he'd still be easy to handle. His girlfriend's out of town an' that's why he's horny. Total bullshit, but Lenny swallowed it whole an' gave the stud his address.

"He'll be here in an hour," he said as he hung up. He was almost gigglin', he was so into it.

"Get hold of it, Lenny," I said, "or you'll fuck it up. Just remember, I'm doin' the job; you're runnin' the camera. That's all till I'm done. Got it?"

He nodded like a monkey in heat, again. An' just a little too quick.

Lenny an' Wayne, there's somethin' about those two, the way they fit each other just a little too perfect, that made me want to call the whole thing off, all of a sudden. I could tell I'm not gettin' the whole picture, here, but it was too late, now; the *stud* was on his way.

Thing is, I got to admit, I — shit, I started feelin' — I dunno...ready for it. I got kind of horny just thinkin' 'bout what I was gonna do to this *rich little college kid* fake fuck. Like I...shit, I missed doin' what I did in prison. It was gonna be just like old times, but this time I'd have somethin' to keep his hands out of the fuckin' way. Make it easier to take total control.

I only had that once, before — havin' a guy tied up so he couldn't fight back. But it was, like, a kick-ass feelin', to the nine-hundredth power. It was when I got a guard at Mid-State. A fuckin' prison guard asshole! *Literally*, like Lenny'd say. Man, that made me feel like I was king of the world.

It happened a week 'fore I was set to go up for a parole hearin'. This overbuilt piece of raw beef in blue had started givin' me shit every time I turned around. His name was Carter an' he was a ten-year military cop vet with this pug-Irish face that made you think of an IRA terrorist. He'd ignored me the two years he worked while I was in, but suddenly he was makin' up for lost time. If my cell wasn't in perfect order, he'd trash it an' make me clean it all up. If my shoes weren't tied, he'd spit on 'em an' make me polish 'em with my shirt. Then he'd bust my balls for wearin' a dirty uniform. If I looked at him wrong, I had to stand at attention an' listen to him bitch for half an hour, usin' words I'd never even *heard* before. An' his guard buddies'd help him when he needed it. Or just wanted it.

'Course, I got what was goin' on; he wanted me to make a move on him so he could fuck up my parole. I just didn't get why. So I figured I'd find out.

First I started actin' like he was gettin' to me, makin' me afraid of him. Wasn't hard to do. Just hunched my shoulders a bit when he came by an' looked away, real quick. Give a little jump when I see him. Swallow hard. All that bullshit stuff. So he started gettin' nastier. Started thinkin' like he *knew* I wouldn't fight back, like I was scared of him. An' he started gettin' stupid an' sloppy about it. After a couple days of that, he was ready to take down. So I made arrangements with a couple of my pack to decoy him into the laundry room 'cause he'd given them some shit, too. Y'know, that's where I was still workin', after *six fuckin' years*! An' Connie wondered why she couldn't get me to do laundry. Anyhow, they had a good idea what I was up to, so they were on board from the get-go.

So 'bout ten a-m, when all the machines were goin', I hid between two of 'em. Sort of a wide space between two packs of washers. Lots of guys slip in there to take care of each other or themselves, but my pack made sure the place stayed clear for me. They waited till the machines were doin' the spin, which gets *real* loud, then one of 'em told him I was in the back gettin' sucked off by my punk of the month. Ol' Carter — big, dumb, blond, full-of-himself Carter — he hustled back there to catch me an' do his number.

Soon as he rounded this corner, he was out of sight of the other guards. That's when I grabbed him, put my little shiv against his throat an' made him come with me way behind the last machine. He was shittin' bricks, lemme tell you, whisperin' the whole way, "C'mon, man, you don't wanna fuck up your parole. You don't wanna do that."

What he didn't get is, I'd learned not to care. You let a fuckin' pig pull shit on you an' get away with it, you lose all the respect you built up inside. An' no fuckin' way was that gonna happen to me.

I slammed his face into this corner an' held him there. Man, I had a hard-on like you wouldn't believe, an' I was pushin' it hard against his ass to let him know what I was gonna do. An' he was freakin', I can tell you. I don't think he really thought I'd do it, 'cause he kept up his bullshit.

"Man, this is stupid. This is stupid. You're already in deep shit. You don't want to add ten years to your sentence!"

I slammed him against the corner, again, an' snarled in his ear, "Why you fuckin' with me, man?"

"I ain't," he said, whimperin'.

"Bullshit! You been on my ass all week. Who's got you gunnin' for me?"

"Nobody!"

I reached 'round an' grabbed his crotch. Squeezed it. He gasped, but I had him so tight an' the shiv so sharp against him, he didn't dare yell. "Don't fuckin' lie to me, cunt! I'll cut your fuckin' balls off!"

He squirmed then finally croaked out, "Buddy of mine. He told me you...you got his nephew. When he was in your cell.

Fucked the kid. Fucked him up. He wants you to stay in."

"What d'you mean I fucked him up?"

"He — he tried to kill himself. He's on tranq's. Twenty-four-hour suicide watch."

"No shit?"

"Yeah. I knew him. He was a good kid, just a little fucked up from drugs. Didn't belong in here. Never should have been sent here. And now..."

"An' it's me fucked him up, huh?"

He nodded. I fuckin' loved it! Really fuckin' loved the idea that I'd messed up some rich-bitch little pansy's life so much that mommy an' daddy had to shell out some of their big bucks to put him back together. I mean, twenty-four-seven care ain't cheap, even if you got insurance. An' I bet I knew which punk it was, too — that first one I hammered in the ass an' got to shoot his wad. He was roistered out 'fore Carter transferred in. I almost came in my pants thinkin' 'bout it.

So fuckin' Carter thought he'd punish me for it. Stupid motherfuckin' Carter was gonna make me pay for doin' somethin' that he let happen a dozen times a day to other people's sons. An' nephews. An' fathers. An' husbands. An' shit. Man, I had to smile at that. Fuckin' hypocrite. He deserved anything I did to him.

I took my hand off his crotch but kept the shiv tight against his throat. He was shiverin'. I could feel him. I think he was more scared of me bein' quiet than of anything else'd happened, so far. He was smart to be.

I pulled a strip from a towel I'd shredded out of my pocket an' whispered to him, "Put your hands behind you."

He jolted an' asked me, "Why?"

I dug the shiv into his neck, just enough to cut him. He gasped then did as I said. I used the strip to tie his wrists together. Twice around. Good an' knotted. Got 'em so tight he grunted from the pain. Then I turned him 'round to face me. I was still smilin', an' that scared him more than anything. Fuckin' shit. A fuckin' guard was shakin' 'cause of me. This was gonna be great.

I crushed him against the corner an' whispered, "How 'bout I show ya what I did to your buddy's nephew?"

"What?" But then it hit him an' he shook his head an' choked out a, "No."

I pressed harder against him. Held him tight against the brick. Ground my dick into his crotch. An' grinned wider. Then I unbuckled his belt. He jolted an' tried to squirm away, so I slammed him to the floor. He landed hard, but he was still able to cry out. He started to scream loud enough he might've been heard over the noise of the machines, so I yanked off my tee-shirt an' jammed it into his mouth. Hard. Almost down his throat. He gagged an' tried to kick me, so I pulled his pants down to his ankles an' pulled his belt tight around 'em. Then I pulled my tee-shirt out of his mouth — didn't want him to choke to death — and used it as a gag on him. Now he was too tied down to do me much damage. He still bucked an' tried to yell, but the noise from the washers an' dryers an' the gag kept anybody from hearin' him. I stood up watched the little pig squirm, lovin' it.

His boxers were still pretty much on, so I straddled his chest an' ripped 'em off him. He was uncut, the fuck, but I wasn't gonna back down, not by that point; I was just gonna hurt him, even more.

I turned an' now was straddlin' his belly, watchin' him try to spit out my shirt an' look around for help an' shake his head, no. I slid my zipper down, slow. Tauntin' him. Then I dug inside an' pulled out my dick. Man, I was hard as a rock. I rubbed it against his face. He shook his head like he was gonna go nuts. I almost laughed.

"This is goin' up your ass, bitch," I said, "an' you're gonna love it. That's what fucked up your buddy's cunt of a nephew — me showin' him how much he liked havin' my thick dick up his sweet little ass."

Carter tried to scream, so I slapped him. Hard. Twice. He started cryin'. I pulled my shirt down from his mouth to around his neck an' twisted it tight. He gasped for air but could still breathe, just not enough to yell. I held it there with my left hand as I unbuttoned his shirt with my right.

He had big pecs, hairless an' smooth, an' his abs were as soft an' smooth as Connie's. Surprised me. I figured he'd have something like the six-packs you see these iron-junkies always goin' for. Not that I gave a shit about how he looked.

He just gasped an' shook his head an' muttered, "No, God, please," over an' over.

I twisted my shirt a little tighter to shut him up. Then I shifted around, pulled his legs up an' slipped between 'em an' lubed myself with some spit. Before he could even think about it, I'd rammed my dick deep into him.

He tried to scream, but I had my shirt twisted too tight 'round his throat, so he just choked. When I was all the way in him, I let it loose a little. Didn't want him hurlin' on me or drownin' in his own puke. Then I pumped into him, long an' slow an' hard. An' I played with his ass. An' I stroked his belly. An' I sucked on his tits. An' I told myself I was back with Connie, fuckin' her an' suckin' on her tits an' rubbin' her belly like I always had. An' finally came the fun part — he started gettin' hard. Soon you couldn't tell he wasn't cut, an' just to prove how much he was my bitch, I let go of my shirt, kept lickin' his tits an' stroking his abs, an' made my other hand circle his dick, an' I began pullin' on it.

He froze, like he couldn't believe what was happenin', then he said, "What th' fuck're you doin'?"

I twisted the shirt tight, again, an' kept pullin' on his dick. He got harder an' harder, an' I sneered as he tried to squirm away from me. I was close to comin', so I slowed down my action an' pulled harder on his dick. Even spit in my hand to make the pullin' smoother. I wanted this fucker to taste his own shit.

After a couple minutes, I was close to firin' into him, an' I was wonderin' if he ever was gonna shoot. He was fightin' me, like you wouldn't believe — shakin' his head an' tryin' to twist away from my hand an' kickin'. But he couldn't do much; each time he got too crazy, I just squeezed his dick hard, like I was gonna tear it off, an' he'd freeze an' let me keep goin'. A couple times he tried to crush me with his legs, but he couldn't get any leverage an' besides, I was too solid built for that to work. I kept pumpin'.

An' pumpin'.

An' pumpin'.

Then just as I was figurin' he's never gonna blow an' I should just let myself finish, he began to buck an' gasp. An' his ass clinched so tight around my dick, I *couldn't* wait anymore; I plowed deep into him an' let loose.

Man...it was scary how good it felt. Just like when I did it the first time to that rich pansy punk's ass. Carter kept fightin' me the whole time, even as I kept plowin' my load into him, an' that made it so...much...better. But it wasn't till I was done an' had pulled out that I realized he'd cum, too. Not much. Just a dribble of sticky stuff leakin' from his dick. But it was enough for me to smear his face with an' tell him, "That's your cum, bitch."

He gagged an' balled up into this little knot an' started sobbin' as he tried to hide his face an' his dick from me. I cut free his hands an' stood up, even though I was still weak in the knees. He whipped his arms around to cover himself, still sobbin'. I watched him...an' I felt this really weird urge. This one'd been so fuckin' good, I knew I could've done it, again, if I'd wanted to. Put him on his belly, this time. Just do it for me an' fuck even tryin' to get him off. I really thought about it, but then I figured, naw, it'd be too much like sex.

I grabbed the torn boxers an' used 'em to wipe off with. Then I tucked 'em into my pants — to throw away later; don't want to leave evidence like that behind — pulled on my tee-shirt an' walked away. Didn't say a word, just left him there. If he said anything, I could say he'd made me fuck him. That's why he was pullin' all his shit — to scare me into givin' him my dick. An' I had lots of witnesses to back up how hard he'd been on me. At best, it'd be his word against mine, even with the bruises on his wrists. But I knew he wouldn't tell nobody. He was too fuckin' ashamed of what'd happened.

An' sure enough, he left me alone, after that. An' I made parole, a week later.

An' here I was, about to do the same thing, again. I was almost sick from excitement.

Lenny must've checked those fuckin' cameras a hundred times before the doorbell rang. They were both the same model an' put out a great picture so long as the lights were right. Oh, an' he made sure every light in the room was on, this time, *just to be sure.*

The plan was simple — Lenny'd let the stud in, make sure the guy knew he was there for sex, then I'd pop out of the kitchen an' grab him. The rest was up to me, but I didn't expect too much trouble. Even if he knew karate or some shit, I could get control before he knew what was happenin'. So when the bell rang, we were ready.

I slipped into the kitchen an' got the straps ready an' peeked out to watch. The front door was in plain sight. Lenny hit the camera's record button an' *strolled* over to the door. He opened it an' stepped back, breathing hard. Whether it was from excitement or fear, I dunno.

I heard the guy say, "Lenny?" an' Lenny answered, "Jeremy? Yeah, come on in."

The guy that entered was probably one of Lenny's an' Wayne's wet dreams. An' he looked familiar. He was taller than me an' maybe older by a couple of years — *college stud,* my ass. He had broad shoulders, dark hair cut short an' neat, an' wore a white cotton shirt an' tight Levi's with a black belt an' black loafers. Hair on his arms an' chest peeked out from under the shirt — not too much, but enough to make him seem like a guy instead of a boy. But swimmer's build? My ass; he wasn't that slim. Or broad shouldered. But he DID look like the poster queen for Gay America. Probably a *gay for pay* closet case. Shit, how hard could it be? Pun intended.

But what was best is, he *did* look a lot like Anthony. His face wasn't as round or as Italian. An' his jaw was stronger. Cleaner. But I could make it work. But then I remembered someone else'd reminded me of that little fuck, an' that's when it hit me — *Jeremy* looked exactly like that guy in *Psycho*. Th' one in the hotel room at the beginnin', who Janet Leigh steals the cash for. Connie took me to see it just after we met. It started out slow as shit, but things picked up in that motel, boy did they. Got me hot as shit for Janet, lemme tell ya. Anyhow, that character was so neat an' clean an' looked so much like a cop, all I could think about when he was on-screen was how much I'd like to smash his squeaky-pretty little face in. Now it looked like I was gonna get that chance.

Jeremy looked around an' said, "Nice place."

Lenny twittered — swear to God — as he said, "Thanks. You want something to drink? Beer, wine, coke, whiskey?"

"Depends on what you're after," Jeremy said, keepin' just out of Lenny's reach.

Somethin' about that set off alarms in my brain. I don't know shit about guys who always go to guys' homes for this kind of sex, but I know enough to know he oughta be doin' somethin' to get Lenny all primed an' ready to want more. An' *Jeremy* was bein' more stand-offish. I put the straps in the *stuff* drawer an' peeked back out.

"What do you think?" Lenny asked.

"I'm not a mind reader."

"Well, I do need to know — are you circumcised?"

"What difference does that make?" the stud asked.

"Well, all the difference," said Lenny, glancing at the kitchen. Dumb fuck. He was probably shitty at poker, too.

The stud eyed him an' said, "I am."

"How much to show me?" Lenny asked.

Jeremy reached down an' dug into his jeans an' pulled out a badge! He was a fuckin' cop! I fuckin' knew it!

"How 'bout I show you this?" he said. "I'm citing you for solicitation of prostitution."

"Oh, shit!" Lenny squeaked — swear to God, he squeaked!

That's when I took a chance an' barged in with a bottle of beer.

"Hey, Wayne, what th' fuck's goin' on?" I asked Lenny, but I was lookin' straight at the cop. "This better be somebody here for big-bad-Lenny, bitch."

The pig jumped an' backed to the door, badge up as he all but screamed, "Hold it, right there!"

I stopped an' looked at him like he was nuts. "What th' fuck's your problem?" I asked, then I called up the stairs, "Hey, Lenny, you steppin' out, tonight?"

Wayne came down, shootin' daggers at me with his eyes. But he got the message. Lenny was all but pissin' in his pants, but Wayne, fuckin' Wayne picked up the slack, beautifully. Right then I knew I'd better take a good hard second look at him, big-time.

"Okay, fine, let's get the jokes over with. So I called a fuckin' escort service?! So fuckin' what? I needed a date."

Jeremy was gettin' real confused, so he opened the door an' yelled for his back-up — two uniforms lookin' like they wanted to bust somebody's balls. I stood stock still in my spot, eyein' all three of the pigs like they were the scum they were, an' I laughed. "Fuckin' shit, Lenny, you called a cop!"

"Bullshit!" said Wayne an' he turned his glare on the stud. "Let me see your badge!"

"Stay where you are!" The stud was about to come unglued. An' now his backup was more confused than ready to break bones.

"What's goin' on, Shayes?" one of 'em asked.

"I dunno," the stud said, "but all these guys're under arrest for soliciting prostitution. An' we're takin' 'em in!"

"You fuckin' kiddin' me?!" I snarled, an' I made it a good one. Jeremy — Shayes looked at me, an' he kept his eyes on me from then on. "I come in th' room after you're already yellin' at my buddy here — "

"Your buddy asked me for sex."

"My buddy ain't asked you for shit, ass-wipe."

"I already got you! He made the request — !"

"You got shit! I was in the kitchen an' I didn't hear Wayne

ask you for one fuckin' thing. He told you to wait an' Lenny'd be right out, that's it."

"It doesn't matter what you say, asshole. What matters is what goes in my report!" Then he motioned to the uniforms. "He's up for resisting arrest."

One of the uniforms started for me, an' I didn't budge. It was Wayne who stopped him, cold. He got real quiet an' said, "All right, arrest us. Take us down to jail. I have an excellent attorney. I have friends at GLAAD and the ACLU. And we have the word of three men versus one. Unless you're wearing a wire. But somehow I don't think you are, seeing as how you're really the cocky sort who just knows any jury'd believe him instead of a fucking faggot. So by this time, tomorrow, we'll have your asses for lunch, an' we won't even need to pay for them."

Shayes gave off just a hint of hesitation, but it was enough for me to pick up on. I smiled an' turned an' put my hands behind my head. The uniform pig went ahead an' frisked me an' was about to twist my hands around to cuff me as he was mouthin' off, "You have the right to remain silent — " But that's as far as he got before I heard Shayes say, "Aw, fuck it! It ain't worth the trouble."

I pulled my hands away from the pig an' turned around to look at Shayes. Lenny got weak in the knees an' sat against the arm of the couch. He was whiter than the stud's shirt. An' *the stud* was redder than my dick, he was so pissed.

"But I still wanna see your identification," he said, tryin' hard to sound like he was still under control an' not doin' a real good job of it.

"No," I said.

"I can demand it," he said, gettin' angrier.

"On the street," I said back. "This is a private home, an' it ain't in fuckin' Georgia, so you wanna pull that shit, you take it outside. You wait till we leave, an' you make up some excuse to stop us an' see what it gets you, then, *officer* Shayes."

Shayes glared at me like he was tryin' to print my face on his brain. Then he looked at Lenny, who looked at me like he was about to puke. Then Shayes looked at Wayne, who just shook his head, stepped back an' leaned against the door's frame. That's when he knew it was an all or nothin' situation; either he busted us an' dealt with the uproar that'd follow or he walked.

The fuck made what looked like the right decision to himself — he walked. He had his uniforms head out, first, then he started after 'em.

But then he was dumb shit enough to look at me an' mutter, "Fuckin' faggots," as he left.

The stupid fuck. If he hadn't said that, I'd of let it drop. I been rousted by cops, before; it's no big deal. But let one call me a faggot? I ain't gonna let it go.

I watched him walk out the door an' down the steps to the street, memorizin' every movement of his body. Even in his jeans an' shirt, in the barely lit darkness, you could tell he was built. Shit, his ass rocked as he walked, smooth an' even, makin' the jeans look like they were part of his skin. The rest of him fit it. Nice an' trim yet solid. Could've been a model for some fag underwear catalog or somethin'.

He got to the street, cast us back a dirty look an' hopped into his unmarked car an' drove away. Then his little piggies followed him in their cruiser.

I turned to ol' Wayne an' said...no, I growled, "Man, he would've been fun."

That's when Lenny bolted for the bathroom an' began praisin' the porcelain gods. It was funny, listenin' to this guy who pushed an' shoved for me to prove my shit, all but begged me to let him tape it an' danced around like a kid under a Christmas tree on Christmas Eve when it was about to happen, suddenly hurlin' his dinner because he'd almost got busted for soliciting. Shit, hadn't the fuck even considered that rape's a felony? Don't matter if you drag a straight guy in off the street or give a back-page guy an invite home an' do more to him than he bargained for — you're *makin'* 'em do what they *don't* want to do. Plain an' simple. What would he've done if we'd got busted for *that*?

That's when I noticed Wayne had been watchin' through the window as Shayes an' his pigs left. An' he had this look on his face — swear to God, he had murder in his eyes.

"Fucking pigs," he said. "They pulled this shit on me, before. When I was walking through that park between Robertson and San Vicente, in West Hollywood. A couple of sheriff's boys, two racist skinhead punks, said I made a pass at them. Like I'd be interested in a pair of ugly homophobic little pricks like them. They arrested me. No mere citation; a full-scale arrest. Fingerprints. Mug shot. Overnight stay in jail. Arraignment. Threatened me with prison. Tried to make me sign a confession. Everything. Like this was Iran or China. But I wouldn't give it to them. I wouldn't say a word. I waited till I hired an attorney and we fought it, in court. Hung the jury. And that's only because I'd never been arrested before in my life. Not even any outstanding parking tickets on my record. The D-A had nothing but those two little pigs, and my lawyer got them to contradict each other, right and left. And three out of six people on that jury still believed that all a gay man wants to do is seduce a straight man. Turn him into another faggot. So there had to be at least a grain of truth to what those fucking little pigs said. Motherfucking closet cases. I've hated breeders, ever since."

He moved back, lettin' the curtain drop, still not lookin' at me an' gettin' more an' more pissed. "My bet is, he gets off on it," he said. "Our Officer Shayes. He gets to wag his dick in our faces then toss us in jail for merely suggesting we want it. Then he goes home to his wife and says, *Honey, I had three men come on to me, today. I could've gotten blowjobs right an' left, so you'd better give me one. Right now. Careful with the teeth, this time. Not that I know how a blow job's supposed to be given, seeing as how I've never been touched by another man.* My bet is, that's how he gets himself up. That's how they all do, these plainclothes vice queens who see gay men as inevitable criminals."

Fuckin' Wayne, shit. He was shootin' off lightnin' bolts

with his words. He was shakin' from the piss rollin' in his head. It changed him completely. Suddenly he wasn't this fat assed faggot too scared to think about comin' on to a guy like me without his buddy, Lenny. Suddenly he was this hot-shot wrestler in the ring screamin' for any other asshole anywhere to come face the poundin' he was gonna give him. He was like fuckin' Tyson pumpin' himself up for fifteen rounds. I couldn't fuckin' believe the change.

Then he turned to me with this little snarl of a grin. A grin that now looked about as mean as mean could get. An' he said, "If I was going to fuck a straight man and make him like it — our Officer Shayes, he's the one I'd choose. He'd be worth any kind of hell that'd follow. Yes. Most definitely. Of course, that's probably what he really wants, so it would make the bet moot. Or would it? After all, that's exactly the kind of dick you and Lenny were chasing, wasn't it?"

I didn't get what he said, exactly, but I knew what he was gettin' at. It was plain as the numbers under my mug shot. It was dreamland come to life for each an' every one of us. An' it made me smile. Wayne looked at me, sort of stunned, a bit wary. But then he smiled right back at me. An' then we started laughin', together. Roarin' with laughter. All but rollin' on the floor, knowin' full well what we were gonna do, next.

"Callin' Officer Sha-ayes."

You motherfucker.

Chapter Five

That night, that's when everything stopped bein' a co-production — like what Lenny called it, once — an' started bein' a full-scale war. When Wayne took over, suddenly we're makin' serious battle plans. Sittin' down an' drawin' up a diagram of how it was gonna go. Just like in a football game. An' Lenny turned into the one who's holdin' back. It would of been funny if Wayne wasn't so fuckin' serious about it.

First he asked me what position I wanted Shayes to be in when I fucked him. Which I thought was a weird thing to ask, but I told him, "I do 'em on their back, legs in the air. It's like fuckin' a girl."

"And you achieve greater penetration, that way," he said in this real snickery kind of way he had.

"I want him to feel it," I sneered back, "so it means somethin' to him. So when I'm done, he knows what happened."

Wayne almost stopped breathin', he got so excited. "What about from behind?" he asked.

"I don't like doin' 'em face down, so much."

"No, no, strung up. Hanging by his wrists? His ankles secured? Are you open to that, as well?"

That sounded weird. "I — I dunno," I said. "I can't picture it."

So he went online with this bondage website to show me what he was talkin' 'bout. I gotta tell ya, I never seen the kind of shit they got out now that you can buy, all of it aimed towards tyin' a guy down so you can do what you want to him. Leather straps. Thick leather gags with things stickin' out of 'em like dildos an' connected by little buckles, like they were sandals for your face, or with little colored balls to stick in their mouth that were from the size of golf balls to baseballs. Harnesses like you'd find on horses. Hammocks to strap a guy to so he could hang in the air when you fucked him. An' that's on top of all the handcuffs an' hoods an' little pouches for God knows what they offered. The only thing I saw that I really understood the use for — I mean, aside from just tyin' a guy down — was a silver cock ring, 'cause this one queen that bought me a few weeks back asked me to wear it while he sucked me off. Took me forever to cum, an' when I did — it was weird.

What Wayne was talkin' 'bout was havin' Shayes hang from the ceiling by a rope or chain, wrists wrapped in some wool-lined leather straps so there'd be no marks, legs held apart by some kind of leather strapped pole buckled to his ankles. They'd be wide enough apart for me to slip 'em over my shoulders an' fuck him standin' up, if I wanted. It'd be sort of like he was on his back.

"I can do it," I said — shrugged, really, "but why not just let me do him on a bed? It's easier."

Lenny nodded when he saw it an' said, "Yeah, you — you'd never get him to cum if — if you do it like that."

I looked at him, wonderin' if he was tryin' to egg me on.

Wayne worked up a sketch of what he wanted to do to a shed they had in their yard behind the condo. He was gonna cover the walls with foam blocks to muffle the sounds an' attach hoops or hooks to the ceilin' to string Shayes up. The only furniture'd be a bed an' dinin' chair to tie Shayes to. Between the mattress an' box springs of the bed, he was gonna lay in these straps that got chrome rings you can loop rope through. They had a picture of this one guy tied to it — spread eagle an' goin' nowhere — that looked kind o' creepy. It also looked like I wasn't the only one gonna have some fun with the fucker. Not that I gave much of a shit about what happened once I was done.

Now I was gettin' to where I knew who Wayne was — in his brain, anyway. The quiet ones, they're always the ones that're plannin', thinkin', figurin' out ways to rock your world in one way or another. I could almost picture him havin' these long talks with himself, plannin' the whole thing out like it really *was* a military campaign then goin' through the actions in his head as he whacked off. Made me wonder if he'd been tryin' to figure out some way to do this to me.

I hoped the fuck wasn't dumb enough to think he could.

It wound up, Wayne got hold of this bondage catalog from the back of some *Tie Me Up* rag to order all the restraints. He told me he did it under a fake name, paid for 'em with a money order an' had 'em sent to this mailbox place on Beverly, where he had a box. Had 'em sent FedEx so the guy at the place'd sign for 'em. Like that'd keep the cops from trackin' him down if they wanted to. He got a blindfold, too, an' he showed me this weird leather gag that had a metal ring in the middle of it.

"What the fuck's that?" I asked him.

"Force the ring between his teeth," said Wayne, usin' Lenny to show me, "tie it in back and, tah-dah — he can't yell, can't speak. And, most importantly, can't bite." Then he stuck his finger in the hole an' poked Lenny's tongue, makin' him gag.

"Ring ain't big enough," I sneered.

"For you, maybe."

"How far you plannn' to go, Wayne?" I asked him.

He looked at me, dead on, an' said, "Oh, as far as I can."

"You don't think we're gonna do a three-way?"

"What's the matter, Curt?" he asked with this freaky little smile. "Is this becoming too queer for you?"

"Yeah," I snapped. "All I wanna do is fuck him up!"

"So do I!" Wayne snapped right back at me. "But I need these things to hold him down as I fuck him! And suck him off! And make him taste my dick! All of it! I need them to help me make him see he's as big a queer as he pretends not to be."

"You're fuckin' crazy, man," I said.

"Am I? Or am I just finally fighting back against these homophobic motherfuckering vice cops with the only weaponry they really understand?"

I must've been lookin' wary or somethin', 'cause he got real nice, sayin', "Don't worry, Curt; I won't even touch him until you're done. That way it won't seem like sex, to you. Hell, I won't touch you throughout the taping."

"Tapin'?"

Then he showed me he bought another camera just like Lenny's an' another VCR. Now THAT freaked me out.

"Three cameras?!" I yelled. "What you fuckin' think you're gonna do!?"

Wayne smirked an' said, "Tape it. Edit it. Sell it on eBay, if I can. Show the world what vice cops really like."

Now I was pissed. "Meanin' people'll see me on it, too, asshole!"

"No, no, no, Curt." That's when Wayne showed me this head mask. He was dolin' out the surprises like they were Halloween candy. "You'll wear this the whole time. And we'll cover your tattoos with makeup. Or change them so you can't be identified."

"Forget it! It's bullshit! I'm not out to make a porno flick! I just wanted to do some damage to the fucker!"

"And that's what we'll do," he said, his voice all gentle an' soothin', again. "Think about it, Curt. What will hurt Shayes more — you putting your dick up his ass? Or his buddies watching you do it? And watching him ejaculate as you fuck him? And then seeing me cum on his face as he sucks me off? Won't that give you even more pleasure? Won't that cause even more damage? All the other guys you've done this to — it's a secret kept between you and them. This time, our boy won't have the option to keep it quiet. I'll send a carefully edited version to vice to let them know *we're mad as hell and we ain't gonna take it no more*."

"Will you say what th' fuck you mean, for once!?"

"I'll tell them we'll do it to their other vice decoys, too. Unless they leave us alone."

"We?!"

"Me. Once I see how you do it, I'll be able to copy you."

"But the cops'll — "

"Yes, the police will grow furious. And they may come looking for me. But many will still wonder if Shayes didn't really seek these pleasures out and wind up caught on tape. This will at least drive him out of vice. As for the rest, they'll begin to wonder if we mean it. And worry that the next time they pull their shit on a fag, they might wind up being taken down by a dozen more of us an' gang-banged in some alley."

It made a weird kind of sense an' — well, that got my warnin' bell goin' off, again. Any time I ever got myself into deep shit, it was by usin' these same kinds of arguments to talk myself into doin' it. That's how I wound up in Mid-State — listenin' to dumb-fuck Terrence convince me that carryin' his baggies of coke wasn't the same as dealin' it.

"You'd just be a mule, man," he said, over an' over. Emphasizin' it was also a quick two bills for nothin'. Over an' over till I swallowed it, whole. That's what me screwed for the rest of my life — *literally*, as Lenny would say.

An' now way deep down somethin' was warnin' me it was gonna happen, again. But it was a tiny voice. A real weak voice. So it was easy to push aside.

An' then Wayne was promisin' me more cash on top of Lenny's offer — lots more. Now I needed both money an' car, real bad, no question. But I got to be honest, here — I liked the idea of screwin' with the cops, again. *Literally.* So I kept on with it.

'Course, that's when Lenny suddenly started tryin' to weasel out of the mess.

"This is getting too crazy," he whined. "It was just a one-time bet and it didn't happen. It wasn't meant to happen, so it's off. It's off."

Wayne sneered at him. "Don't play so innocent, Lenny. You were all set to partake of Officer Shayes when he was just *Jeremy*, so you're part of this, too. You don't have to join in the festivities; you can just run the cameras, but you'll be there the whole time. It's your punishment for almost getting us arrested."

"It's my car," said Lenny. "And my camera. I won't let it happen. I'm the one who'll have to sign the title over, and you wouldn't know how to run a camera if you took a six year course in it, so forget it."

I thought Wayne was gonna have a stroke, he got so red. He yanked Lenny off to one side an' said some things to him I couldn't hear — but that I could sure tell were *not* nice or pretty. Then he came back to me.

Lenny stayed away, sittin' on the same couch arm he'd sat on when Shayes first tried to bust us, lookin' like he was about to cry. He never tried to stop us, again.

For sure I was gonna keep my eye on Wayne.

I also started keepin' a low-key eye on Shayes. I was perfectly set up for it — workin' nights off an' on an' things gettin' nastier an' nastier between me an' Connie. Seemed like she was yellin' at me more an' more. An' for nothin', most of the time. We weren't fuckin' like we used to, so I guess she was findin' out that's all we had in common, or somethin'. Not that I gave a shit. I mean, her doin' the cunt-wagon got me to hatin' her. An' every time I went to Wayne's, I wound up with a blow job from him or Lenny an' a hundred bucks in my pocket. It got to where that was better than sex with her'd ever been. I mean, not physically, but financially. That's all. Same for emotionally, from either side. In fact, the only good thing about her goin' on the rag was, it gave me an excuse to bust out of the house.

As for Shayes, he was too fuckin' easy. He worked the late shift, got off at midnight or just before. I followed him home, one night — it was easy cake, even in the dark — an' wrote down his address. Up in Woodland Hills. Pricey, but not too much so. I went back a couple times over the next two weeks to scope it out, an' found out from sneakin' a look at his mail that his full name's Jonathan Robert Shayes. *The third*. An' I caught on to how he's got a wife an' three kids — two girls an' a boy, none of 'em in grade school, yet — two cars an' a membership at this gym in Van Nuys. He'd drop off there to pump iron, shower an' shave before headin' to work, four days a week. Like clockwork.

Wayne got a buddy of his at some TV news station to pull up some of Shayes' arrest reports, both before an' after our encounter. The bastard busted a couple dozen guys over the space of a month with the same routine — them callin' him up, him goin' over an' then writin' 'em up or slappin' the cuffs on 'em. A couple were guys from out of town. Probably away from the Mrs. for a sales job an' thought they'd have some fun in La-La land doin' what they really wished they were doin' back home. An' wound up gettin' fucked over for it. So they'd plead *no contest* an' pay their fines as quietly as they could an' hoped nobody'd find out.

Now, I didn't like Shayes, no question, but I didn't hate him, at first...not like Wayne seemed to. Watchin' him drive his year old Ford an' mow his lawn in ratty old GAP shorts an' skanky tee-shirt an' wave at people in the neighborhood an' play with his kids an' his dog an' his cop buddies when they came over for a barbeque — he just made me tired. Beyond belief. He was a nothin' guy in a nothin' world doin' a job bustin' guys who tried to forget they had nothin' lives, too.

But readin' those reports? Seein' how they all read the same, almost down to the word? Knowin' it meant it didn't matter what did or didn't really happen, that when Shayes went off on his little visits, it was with the sole intention of bustin' up somebody's life 'cause they weren't what the world saw as acceptable? Well, I started hatin' him, too.

I started seein' in him all the assholes who ever put me down. Who told me how to live then turned their backs on me when I tried to be like they wanted. Who punished me for not just lettin' 'em kill what little fire I had inside me. Who let others try to tear me apart to prove I was breakable. Who just vanished from my life. He was those guards on my first night in prison, who put me in a cell with three beaners knowin' full well they'd fuck me in the mouth an' in the ass. He was that fuckin' minister who told me to live by God's word then didn't do a fuckin' thing to help me do it when I was freed. He was that fuckin' dealer who gave me my first drag on a doobie then got me to workin' for him so I could afford to keep doin' it, 'cause it helped me not to care. He was Connie always ridin' my ass 'bout not doin' better with my life. He was my mom for not bein' my mom. He was her asshole husband. He was fuckin' Anthony. He was shit, to me, an' I was gonna show him just how shit gets treated.

An' I was gonna make it worth prison.

We decided the best time to take the fucker was before he hit the gym. Nobody'd notice he wasn't there, so he wouldn't get missed till he didn't show for work, an' by then we'd be havin' our fun with him. I had it worked out how to grab him, all Wayne had to do was drive the van.

Shayes always left his house right between one an' one-fifteen, so me an' Wayne were ready an' waitin' by that time. I wanted us to be down by the gym, waitin' for him there. I knew what his car looked like an' where he usually parked it, but Wayne had this need to see him come out of his home.

"Preparation," he called it.

I didn't get it. Didn't like it, but then he pointed out somebody might see us waitin' for Shayes an' get suspicious; better if we follow him like a couple guys who just happen to be goin' the same way as him. I still didn't like it, but I went along.

So there we were, half a block down in an empty subdivision. Waitin'. I dunno 'bout Wayne, but my heart was poundin' an' I could barely sit still, I was so up for it. I kept tryin' to figure out how things could go wrong an' lay plans to take care of that. My only real worry was if he had a pistol in his car. I hadn't seen him carry one with him to the gym, but bein' a cop, for sure he had to have one...somewhere. What if he pulled it when I went for him? I wasn't worried about gettin' shot; I was worried I might go off an' kill him. Or get Wayne killed. I mean — yeah, Shayes may be worth prison, but nobody's worth the needle. I did my best to keep thoughts like that out of my head.

But Wayne, shit, he just sat there behind the wheel, hummin' some kind o' sixties tune I couldn't quite make out, not lookin' at anything. It sort of ticked me off, 'cause I was wonderin' if he really understood what we were about to do. No,

I was wonderin' if he really *cared*. That's what's dangerous 'bout doin' the crime — not carin' about gettin' caught. That's when you fuck up an' lead the cops straight to ya. An' me, I'm a one-timer, already so I didn't want to go down with a second strike. Or third, the way some DAs'd screw around with the law. So after a couple minutes of Wayne's non-music, I was close to tellin' the fuck to shut up an' pay attention; but then he stopped all on his own.

I looked at him, an' all of a sudden he looked really tired an' — I dunno, sad. No, not sad. Stunned. Like he'd just seen somethin' A car wreck of disaster that he couldn't take in.

"Curt," he asked in this voice so soft I almost couldn't hear it, "do you ever wonder at what you're capable of? At what you're really truly capable of doing?"

That spooked me. An' relieved me, a little. Maybe WAYNE was gonna back out — which I almost wouldn't have minded.

I shrugged an' said, "Crazy question. Especially now."

"Yes, it is. You know, I'll be forty-six in three days, an' I'll see it as a grandfather."

That jolted me. "What?"

"My oldest had her first child a couple months ago. A boy. Kendall. *Ken Doll*. I doubt she caught the irony when she christened him."

"Wait, wait, wait — whoa. Oldest? *Daughter*? As in more than *one*?"

He gave me a smirk. "How observant you are. I have four. Well, *had*. I was forbidden contact with them once my wife learned I liked men more than I did her."

"Shit, Wayne."

"To put it mildly. It was not the sweetest of divorces. What's funny is, I can understand why she was so upset. I'd kept it such a good secret for so many years, both before an' during our marriage."

"Why?"

"C'mon, Curt — even in Los Angeles there are large

pockets of fag haters. In the great Midwest, there are entire states of them. If you want to be accepted by people, do business with people, get ahead in any way, you have to be like them — big dumb breeders who think art is a Norman Rockwell poster framed on their wood-paneled living room wall. But if you're careful, if you toe the line, even if they have their suspicions — so long as you have a wife and four children they'll never say anything. Unless you're fool enough to try something with one of their teenaged sons. And there were a couple... "

"That what got you caught?"

"Not exactly. I was smarter than that. I owned two store franchises from a company in Texas. I had to go down every now and then, so I bought a small house on a nearby river. Not far from a good-sized university. I was thirty pounds lighter, then, all of it muscle. I ran ten miles a day. I never had trouble picking a college boy up. That's where I met Lenny, you know. He was doing his Master's in Theater Arts. When we moved out here, he actually built up a nice little resume on television and low-budget features. He was even up for an Emmy, once, and I think a Spirit Award, though I can't swear to that."

"What happened?"

"Oh, one of the students I picked up freaked out and accused me of rape. It was just his word against mine, but I was still arrested and threatened with prison. My wife was called and told all about it by the local police. The charges wound up being dropped; it seems the boy in question had drug problems and was put in rehab by his parents. But I still lost my family. My businesses. Everything but the house in Texas. Once my wife knew what it was for, she didn't want anything to do with it. So I sold it and moved here. Lenny came with me. We started over, together. That was seventeen — no, eighteen years ago."

"Shit, Wayne, you were younger 'n me, now."

"I was never younger than you."

"Wait, dude — wait, you had four kids; when did you get married, twelve?"

"When I graduated college. My 23rd anniversary would

have been last Monday. I sent my ex flowers. My *fuck you* to the bitch."

"Shit, Wayne." Knowin' this sort of spooked me. An' got me to wonderin' too much about what we were plannin', so I had to ask him, "You answer me a question?"

"If I can."

"Be honest?"

He looked at me, that *I know what you're up to* look flashin' cross his face. "What is it, Curt?"

"You've never done this, before?"

"What we're doing now?"

"Anything like what we're doin' now." Like to that kid that accused him.

Wayne looked at me with this expression I couldn't read. I didn't budge, but lemme tell ya, I was ready in case he tried any kind of bullshit on me.

"Why do you ask?" It was more a statement than a question, but I went ahead an' took it as one.

"You're too cool about it," I said. "It's got me just wonderin'. Wonderin' how much practice you've had."

He smiled. "You should see me on the inside. I'm a quaking mass of nerves. I told you my story to keep my mind off this. And to remind myself of why I'm doing it."

"Okay. But you ain't answered my question."

"You mean, did I do it to that boy? Force him to have sex with me?"

"C'mon, man."

"Are you looking for an excuse to back out?"

"Little late for that..." but not too late, added the little voice in my brain.

"True." He looked at me, dead on. "No, I didn't. I haven't. Ever. I swear. Double-dog swear, even."

He was lyin'. I could tell by how tight in control he was of his voice. His words. His actions. But it was too late; that's when Shayes popped out the front door.

He was wearin' his favorite ratty shorts an' tee-shirt, thick white socks an' Nikes already on, gym bag in one hand, hanger with fresh clothes in another.

Wayne perked up a little an' said, "My God, your legs are better than I imagined. But, honey, drop the shorts."

What the fuck? Was he tryin' to be funny?

"What're you on about?" I asked.

"They're ugly," he snapped back. "I realize breeders don't have much clothes sense, but any idiot could see those baggy long khaki things make even the best legs look stunted. It's a disgrace to human anatomy."

Shit, fuckin' Wayne. Bitchy like always. All I could do was laugh an' shove aside what I'd just learned about him.

Shayes dumped his bag in the trunk an' set the hanger in its hook in the car, hopped in an' drove off. Shit, just like clockwork. Fucker never even glanced at us.

Wayne followed him, an' I got to admit — he was like ice the whole time. Drove like a guy out for a drive, not like he was tailin' somebody. But he kept us right behind Shayes for over a mile, makin' every turn the guy made, not changin' lanes even when Shayes did, an' never losin' sight of the guy till I made Wayne take a short cut, one I found out so Shayes wouldn't have reason to notice us followin' him. I mean, we knew where he was headin'; better to get there first.

We parked at a meter two blocks down from the gym just a couple minutes before Shayes' Ford zipped past. He was goin' faster than we thought he would, so Wayne had to peel out to follow him, an' we almost got side-swiped by this truck that came out o' nowhere. It honked an' the guy flipped us off, but Wayne kept his cool. He just shrugged a *sorry* at him then caught up to Shayes at the next light.

The gym had a parkin' lot, but nine times out of ten it was packed to the point where people were sittin' idlin' in their cars, waitin' for somebody to pull out, so Shayes usually put his car on this residential area nearby. That way he didn't have to feed a meter. Those streets were lined with trees an' had lots of bushes an' not much traffic. It was perfect.

He drove on down to the street an' turned, never once lookin' at us. Wayne slowed down as we turned after him, so we could pull on some ski masks to hide our faces.

Shayes parked a block down, behind this huge SUV an' popped his trunk from the inside. That's when Wayne slowed down even more to let me out, then he stopped right by Shayes' car, so close the cop couldn't open his door or see inside the van. Then I snuck around to the other side.

Shayes noticed the van an' honked his horn, irritated. "Hey, hey, I'm trying to get out!"

He didn't even notice me till I'd yanked the door open. The dumb fuck left everything unlocked when he drove! All Shayes could do was jump an' say, "Holy shit!" 'fore I had one of Wayne's carvin' knives to his throat an' was pressin' him hard against the door. His eyes got so big an' wide, I could see white all around as I whispered, "Shh. Shh — one word an' you're dead."

He put his hands up an' whispered, "Okay, man. Okay." Wayne drove the van out of the way, then I forced Shayes out through the driver's door.

He moved like he was readin' my thoughts. "Get out. Nice an' slow. Don't move too sudden. I'm followin' ya so be careful." I moved out with him. He was shakin' so he stumbled a bit. I grabbed him with my free hand. I still cut his neck a little — by accident — but that was the only problem. One back door to the van swung open an' Wayne yanked him inside. I jumped in, after them.

That's when Shayes realized this wasn't just some plain ol' muggin'. He jolted an' jammed Wayne back against the truck's seats, but before he could turn on me, I grabbed him by the hair an' yanked him against me. Then I put the knife to his throat an' snarled, "Pull that shit again an' I'll slice your fuckin' head off, motherfucker."

He froze, mutterin', "What the fuck?" over an' over.

I held the knife as Wayne scurried over an' wrapped the plastic strap 'round his ankles. Then he forced this dildo-gag into

Shayes' mouth. The fucker didn't want to take it, but I slit the skin by his Adam's Apple — deliberately, this time — an' he let Wayne put it on him. Then I rolled him onto his belly an' Wayne tied his hands together an' strapped the blindfold 'round his eyes. He was bleedin' a little from the two cuts, but nothin' serious.

When he was done, I scrambled back an' grabbed the gym bag from the Ford's trunk an' scrambled back into the van. The second I closed the door, Wayne jumped in the driver's seat, whipped off his ski mask an' calmly drove away. Took us a total of forty seconds, if that. So far, so good.

He drove fast but careful, not exactly like a typical L-A driver. I mean, they are the freaks, out here. We turned back onto Van Nuys an' hit down to the one-oh-one. The plan was to head for the Cahuenga Pass then to go down Highland to Sunset an' back to the condo. Just a van on the road in the middle of the afternoon, nothin' special about it.

"Rather like William Bonin," Wayne'd said me when he plotted it out. I had zero idea of who he was, so he told me, "A local man who did something similar about twenty-five years ago, albeit with teenaged boys instead of men."

My only response was, "Gross." Wayne had nodded in agreement. But I noticed he knew all about the guy.

Anyway, I stayed in the back to watch Shayes to make sure he didn't try anything. An' seein' him lie there — face down, his legs tied at the ankles with a strap, his hands strapped behind him at the wrist, his eyes an' mouth invisible behind the gag an' blindfold — it made me feel...I dunno, easy. Strong. I mean, I could do anything I wanted to this guy, right now, an' here I was just sittin' here watchin' him. Noticin' how his shorts had rode up to reveal his briefs on one side. An' how one arm of his tee shirt had gotten almost torn off — when, I don't remember. An' how the hair on his legs lay flat against his skin, like mine.

I saw how he'd taken off his weddin' ring — so he could hit on the pump-bunnies at the gym, I guess — an' how his fingernails looked neat an' clean but not too perfect. An' how his feet weren't all that big but his calves were. As I sat there, I dug through his gym bag an' found his wallet. Rifled through it an' saw he was thirty-one, weighed 185, had brown hair an' blue eyes, an' was an Aries. I looked at pictures of his wife an' kids, all perfectly posed, an' counted out eighty bucks in cash that went straight into my pocket. On top of it all, he had two credit cards an' full insurance coverage. A real stand-up guy in the *real* community.

His bag held socks, briefs, tee shirt, towel, all *Springtime fresh* — soap, deodorant, sandals, workout gloves, sweat rag, pack of DoubleMint gum.

An' his pistol, buried at the bottom.

His badge was there, too, gold an' shiny an' big. I smiled, knowin' full well he'd never get these back. Then I just sat there, watchin' him. An' feelin' how soft that fuckin' towel was.

It's weird — but that towel hurt me. Gave me a pain deep inside. I dunno why, but I held it close. Smelled it. Let it go smooth over my skin. Lay it gentle 'round my neck. I'd never felt a towel like that, before. Even Connie, who knows her materials an' how to wash 'em, not even she ever had a towel like this. So rich an' beautiful. But he had it. That motherfucker had it. Fuckin' shit, he had it. An' I couldn't stop caressin' it. An' what's funny is, even though I had it, I couldn't say it was mine. It was too alien to me. So all I could do was keep touchin' it as I watched Shayes.

It took him a few minutes to calm down, he was breathin' so hard an' shiverin' so much. But then I could almost see the gears start workin' in his head, tryin' to figure out what the deal was. Why we'd grabbed him. Where we were goin'. Anything he could make out in spite of the blindfold. He started to mutter stuff — things like, "Hey...hey...is somebody there?" an' "What's going on?" His voice was muffled an' garbled an' hard to understand, but I could pretty much make out what he was sayin'.

Fuckin' movies — they make you think puttin' a gag on somebody shuts 'em up, but it don't. They can still yell an' chatter an' make plenty of noise. I always had to laugh when some *bad guy* would put his hand over the heroine's mouth to keep her quiet. I tried that once with Connie an' she only screamed louder an' nastier, an' nearly bit a finger off.

So here was Shayes, his little cop brain goin' ninety to nothin', tryin' to talk to somebody, tryin' to figure out what he can do to get back in control. But he was gone, lemme tell ya. Didn't know it yet, but he was mine. An' I was startin' to enjoy just sittin' there, holdin' that towel an' quietly watchin' him squirm.

After a couple minutes, he scrunched together an' started tryin' to sit up. The van was jerkin' an' rollin' a little an' it screwed him up a little, but he finally got to where he was leanin' against its side. Then he sort of tried to look around under the blindfold. I knew I was out of his line of sight, if he had any, but I was close enough in case he tried somethin'.

His legs were bent, an' it struck me how good of a shape they *did* have. Nice form. Muscled. Not too built up like mine were gettin' to be. Not too short or too long. Good clean skin. Nothin' sharp or harsh to 'em. A real guy's legs. Perfect legs for this perfect towel. An' why the fuck was I noticin' that? Why the fuck was I even THINKIN' that? Shit.

I made myself put down the towel an' then I rubbed my eyes. I kept my focus on Shayes as he worked at the straps 'round his wrists. I shook my head. Fuckin' cop'd used the same fuckin' things so many times in the past an' nobody'd gotten loose; why'd he think he could get out of 'em? It was almost funny to watch.

Pretty soon, we were gettin' off at Highland. He could feel us slowin' down. Feel us jumpin' over that bumpy little bridge of an exit an' swingin' down to connect with the road just above the Bowl. He got real still.

Too still.

I got ready an', sure enough — when we stopped at a light, he began poundin' his back against the side of the van, screamin' at the top of his lungs!

I was on him, in a flash! I yanked him back onto the van's floor, straddled his gut an' rammed a forearm across his neck! He shut up, real quick.

"Try that, again," I whispered, "you're dead."

"Please, don't do this," he muttered from behind the gag. "Just let me go. You don't have to do this."

I just smiled. That's when I realized I could feel him breathin' hard between my legs. Feel him squirmin' 'cause his arms were pinned under him an' his shoulders were strainin' at the position. I'd torn his shirt when I yanked him down. Not much, just enough to show he had some full pecs an' they had flat swirls of hair over 'em, just like his legs an' arms. No way was I ever gonna think of Connie when I was doin' this guy. But I still started breathin' hard. An' my dick still got goin' good.

I don't know why, but I shifted down to where I was restin' on his hips. I guess it was to take some pressure off his shoulders. He squirmed an' stretched as best he could an' rose up to rest on his elbows. The bottom of his shirt had ridden up, some, so I could tell he had decent abs, no six-pack but solid an' covered with some hair. An' sittin' on him like that, completely in control — I wanted to touch him.

I slipped a hand up to his pecs. Yeah, solid muscle. He jerked but couldn't do much more. I pulled the tee shirt open some more where it was torn — not too much; Wayne wanted to *undress* him on camera — an' saw one of his tits. It was brown an' soft an' hair swirled around it. I played with it, a little. Shit, even when I closed my eyes, I could still feel the hair. Be even more obvious when I sucked on it.

He really began to squirm, then. "What — what's goin' on? What're you doin?"

"What the fuck you think, faggot?" I snarled.

Then I leaned back an' let my hands go down his legs an' drew 'em back up, pullin' one shorts' leg up with it. He tried to buck me off, but I smacked my legs against his sides, knockin' the wind out of him. He stayed still, tryin' to catch his breath. Then I shifted around to straddle his chest an' looked down at his crotch. An' I unzipped his shorts an' saw he's wearin' white Haynes or Jockeys or somethin' generic, like that. Nice an' clean, too.

I could just hear Shayes whisperin', "Please, please, you don't want to do this. I'm not that way. Please. I got a wife. I got kids. I — I haven't seen you. Any of you. Please, just let me go. I — I won't report it. Please."

"Don't worry," I whispered, caressin' his belly. "We're just gonna have some fun."

Then I pulled his briefs up away from his dick, an' saw he was small an' clean an' cut. Just like he promised.

He tried to wiggle away, so I let his briefs snap back into position an' shifted 'round on him, again, to where I was lyin' on top of him. Man, my dick was poundin' against my jeans, beggin' to get out. An' he could feel it grindin' against his own. I held him tighter, like I was comfortin' him. I could feel how quick he was breathin'. I could feel his heart poundin'. I could smell some kind of stuff on him, like Brut or Old Spice mixed in with his own sweat — the kind of sweat that still smells clean, still smells alive. An' I owned him, right then. He was mine, pure an' simple. Completely mine.

"Jesus, Christ," he muttered, "please — please don't hurt me."

"We won't," I said.

Then Wayne turned onto his street an' slowed down, even more, an' turned down an alley. He pulled up to his back gate an' stopped. The shed's door was right beside it. Lenny was there, waitin'.

I could still hear Shayes whisperin', "Please, really, you don't want to do this. I'm not like that. It won't be any good. Please, just let me go. I — I won't do anything to you. Please."

Then Wayne yanked open the side door an' it slid to a loud stop. Shayes gulped an' started heavin'. Wayne noticed.

"Sit him up," he said. "Head between his legs. We don't want him puking into the gag; he might choke." I did what he said, then Wayne climbed in an' put an arm on Shayes' back an' whispered, "Hold on. Get back in control. Breathe deep. Don't talk. Don't even try. If you do, you'll vomit."

Shayes tried real hard to get back in control...but he wasn't havin' much luck. So Wayne pulled out a bandana an' wrapped it around Shayes' neck, then he undid the gag.

"Coke," was all Wayne said. A second later, Lenny had a can of it an' was offerin' it to him. Wayne took it, pulled Shayes back by the bandana an' forced some of it down his throat. The guy choked an' coughed, but he stopped heavin'. "Better?"

After a second, Shayes nodded.

Then Wayne coiled the bandana tighter an' said, "Don't even try to call for help. Understand?"

Shayes nodded, again.

That little action made me positive Wayne was lyin' 'bout not doin' this, before. Maybe he hadn't with a guy like Shayes, maybe it was just that college kid or with some punk he picked up in a bar or off Santa Monica or even paid to let him do it, but he'd done this, before. I mean, I could palm all the other crap — the careful plannin', the wild imagination, the way he wanted the string him up — all of it on just bein' caught up in the idea of it. Even after his story, I couldn't have said for positive he was lyin' to me. But knowin' how to keep this guy from lettin' hurl an' doin' it without much of a thought — he's had practice. What's weird is, that calmed me down. An' it made me even more careful when I was around him.

He kept hold of the bandana as I picked Shayes up to carry him out. The cop struggled a little — not much — but I still felt strong carryin' him into the shed. He's not exactly a little guy, an' holdin' him like you do a bride — I even felt...oh, I dunno, just plain powerful. It was all good. From the shape of his legs to how smooth an' healthy his skin felt to even the hair on his calves ticklin' the hair on my arm — it was all just right. An' havin' the side of his butt pressin' just above my crotch, it got me close to shootin' in my briefs.

Shit, y'know, I — I could tell this was gonna be too fuckin' good. It was gonna be like that first kid an' that guard at Mid-

State, Carter. An' I — I knew I shouldn't be feelin' like that. I mean, I'm straight; I really am. I love pussy an' need the feel of a chick in my bed, at night. An' I knew, even then, I knew I was headin' over the edge. I knew I should've stopped myself, right then. But I — I — I couldn't; swear to God, I couldn't. It was like I was addicted to some kind of drug an' all I could think about was my next fix. Like some low-life junkie piece of shit an' that ain't me.

That ain't me.

But even as I was thinkin' all this, I was still carryin' him into that shed. An' I — I couldn't stop. 'Cause deep down — way deep where you never even think to go — I needed to own him. An' I couldn't do that till I owned him whole.

You couldn't have convinced me of this at the time, but now I can see that I was completely, totally an' absolutely out of control. I was workin' like off auto-pilot or like I was some fuckin' puppet bein' cared around by invisible strings attached to its own brain. An' that brain wasn't at all interested in anything normal or human or acceptable, anymore. It just wanted to be fed some ice cold revenge an' it'd keep yankin' at me till it got what it wanted.

An' that made me one scary motherfucker.

Even to myself.

Chapter Six

This was the first time I'd been in Wayne's shed. Shit, it was the first time I was really in his back yard. When he'd been talkin' 'bout makin' the shed over, he only showed it to me through the slidin' glass doors that lead to a two foot wide patio an' two inch patch of grass between the condo an' the fence. I think it used to be a garage, since it was big enough for two small cars. There were two windows an' one door, all inside the fence. The wall facin' the alley was solid an' covered with ivy, an' it crouched in a corner of the yard as if it was leanin' against the fence an' just darin' you to make it leave. It looked nice an' plain an' simple, almost homey, not like a prison. But hey, that's what it was gonna be.

The gate swung to the right an' the door was there on its left, already ajar. Lenny kept the gate open as Wayne guided me in, usin' the bandana to keep control of Shayes, then we slipped into the shed an' Lenny closed the gate an' joined us inside.

I dunno what I expected, exactly, when Wayne told me 'bout what he was gonna do to the place — but what I saw stopped me, cold. First I saw the bed — a big unfinished-wood four-poster jammed against a wall, its mattress covered with a ratty fitted sheet, nothing else. Handcuffs were connected to each corner post an' laid out nice an' neat, waitin' to be clamped onto Shayes' wrists an' ankles. An' two leather restraints were fastened to a thick dowel that ran between the head posts, to keep his hands above his head some of the time. It made me stop an' blink at how harsh it looked.

Then I noticed a heavy steel cable hangin' in the middle of

the room. It had a ring on one end that wasn't completely closed, an' it slipped through a couple of hooks in the ceilin' then connected to a sort of pulley bolted to the floor in a corner opposite the bed, so you could raise or lower how high it was. Beside that was a solid wooden chair, an' next to that was a four-foot tall metal sawhorse padded with leather. An' then coils of rope on the floor. An' then some rolled up foam rubber pallets. All nice an' neat.

The walls were covered with all kinds of misshapen bits of foam in all sorts of colors — gray, yellow, pink, white, you name it — even over the windows. They covered the ceilin', too. Both Wayne's an' Lenny's cameras were already set up on tripods — one on a short platform, the other in a nearby corner — an' the lights were bright. I think the only reason the place wasn't like an oven was 'cause an air conditioner fitted in the wall was goin' full blast.

Now all of this was sort of expected — I'd seen the bondage rags Wayne creamed over; seen his diagrams an' sketches — but that freak must've thought I was a complete an' total blind idiot or somethin'. 'Cause I could tell the second I saw the set-up that none of it was new. Not one fuckin' thing in that room. The bedposts were dull an' worn where the handcuffs had rubbed against them. The ring on the chain was scratched. The metal post was dinged in a couple places. The chrome on the legs of the sawhorse was scraped. The wooden floor was scuffed from the chair bein' dragged over it, an' the chair's stain an' polish were faded an' chipped. They'd used this room before, an' not just once or twice.

Suddenly I was feelin' really — weird. Like I had tiny little sugar ants crawlin' up an' down my arms an' legs an' over my body. Something about that room was wrong — way too fuckin' wrong — an' I just wanted to get the fuck out, but I couldn't move.

Wayne noticed me hesitatin' so he pointed to the bed. "Toss him there an' leave him. I want to savor this moment."

I looked at him. Then looked at the bed. Then remembered

I was carryin' Shayes an' while he wasn't strugglin', he wasn't exactly what you'd call a lightweight, either. I wandered over to the bed an' let him drop onto it. He bounced onto his stomach an' started to roll around — tryin' to get comfortable, I guess, since he knew he wasn't goin' nowhere. I watched him, for a second. Watched him realize he was on a bed an' understand what was gonna happen. What was really gonna happen. An'...an' I gotta hand it to the guy — he didn't give up. He scooted 'round to sit up an' try to see through the blindfold, an' he started yammerin', fast an' breathless, "Listen, listen, you don't understand. I'm a cop. I keep a tight, steady schedule. People're going to be looking for me, soon. Someone may've seen your van and they'll tell the police and it'll be ten times worse for you if you've hurt me in any way, if you've done anything to me. So, let me go, please. Be smart about it. I'll walk away. No harm, no foul. Okay? Okay?"

Wayne just snickered, an' that's when it washed over me like cold ocean water. This whole set-up, this whole plan, this whole room — revenge against a cop had nothin' to do with it. Neither did loneliness or the world's hypocrisy or his own sense of injustice. An' gettin' a homophobe like Shayes to enjoy what he said he hated — that was all a lie. This...all of this...it was just another fuck to Wayne an' Lenny. It was just sex.

How the fuck could I have missed that? Was I that fuckin' blinded by my own need for revenge? Was I that closed off to the idea that maybe I was bein' used to get a couple of perverts a guy they could never get on their own? Was I that fuckin' stupid?

I looked at Wayne like I'd never seen him before. He was standin' to one side of the bed, watchin' Shayes move around an' chatter the same crap, over an' over. An' he was rubbin' his own chest an' crotch. An' boner; it was really showin' in his pants. Lenny was standin' on the other side, almost lickin' his lips. There wasn't any hate or hurt or fear or confusion in their eyes, now; all that was there was just plain lust.

So that's all it was. Those fuckers were usin' me — no,

usin' my anger to help 'em get their rocks off, that's all. Not a damn thing more. I started to breathe almost as fast as Shayes, an' I almost felt sorry for him.

Oh, man, I had to get out of that room.

I tried to back to the door, nice an' slow, but Wayne noticed an' came over to me, askin', "What's wrong?"

I almost froze...then I muttered, "I — I need a beer. Or some fresh air. I guess."

Wayne looked at me. "You're not backing out? Not now."

"No, man," I whispered, barely able to talk. "It's just this — this room; it's freaking me out. No windows. One door. Those cameras."

"Does it remind you of prison?" I'd swear there was a gleam in his eye when he asked me that. "I understand. There's a cooler on the patio with some ice cold Beck's in it, just for you. Why don't you have one. Or two? Have a smoke. Relax. We'll get things ready for you."

I nodded, just wantin' out. Just wantin' away from Wayne's voice. From Shayes' non-stop beggin'. I backed to the door, opened it behind me an' slipped outside. As I closed the door, I saw Wayne'd turned back to the bed, an' he told Shayes, "Don't waste your voice, gorgeous. You're ours, now."

I stumbled over to the patio, tryin' to calm my brain down. Hell, just calm my breathin'. I found the cooler an' popped a Beck's an' downed it in one gulp. Didn't even notice it. I grabbed another one an' had half that into my belly before I took a breath. Then I leaned against this post an' tried to sort things out. Tried to stop shakin'.

You see — an' this ain't no time for lies — I...I really honestly *wanted* to fuck Shayes.

Way down deep, I wanted it.

An' yeah, one reason I was doin' it to get even for all the crap in my life. To do some damage. But that wasn't all there is to it. I — I'd gotten to where I *liked* the feel of my dick up a guy's ass. Liked the way his balls'd rub against my pubes. Liked bein' able to get him off, especially when he didn't want to an'.

An' I looked at guys different because of it. When Shayes left, that night, I remember noticin' how nice his ass was.

Yeah, I told myself it's cause I wanted to fuck him up, but there really was more to it than that. Same for that stud outside the *A Club*. Yeah, I wanted to hurt 'em but I...I wanted to hold 'em, too. I wanted 'em to be mine. Couple of good-lookin' guys, both of 'em. An' that made me happier to be after 'em. Wantin' 'em. Needin' 'em. If that makes any sense. An' that fuckin' room. An' it bein' all set up to let me do whatever I fuckin' wanted. An' it bein' so fuckin' obvious it was just there for sex. It made me see what I was doin' — part of what I wanted to do — was just be with 'em. No matter what. An' I didn't care how much it was gonna fuck the guy up. 'Cause mingled in with all of this was just how much I *liked* holdin' a guy, even when I'm rapin' him.

What the fuck was wrong with me?!

That's fuckin' nuts! I...I...I'm straight!

I'm fuckin' straight!

Ain't I?

Shit, before motherfuckin' Paco an' his boys did me in County, I'd only been with girls. Only liked girls. Only wanted girls. Never even thought about bein' with a guy. I loved — *love* the way girls move an' smell an' fit my hands an' mold into my body. I loved — *love* slippin' my dick into their pussy an' suckin' their tits an' screwin' till dawn. Me an' Connie, we could've wrote the book about sex between a man an' woman. Hell, sometimes I could get off just lookin' at a chick if she was pretty. Like Connie. But since Mid-State...

Man, I gotta admit, after six years there — I got to where I was just as happy with one of my punks. An' yeah, I know, I know — I was makin' 'em do things with me. But they still felt right. It all felt right. It felt just as real as with a girl. So does that make me a fag? Did Paco — hell, did fuckin' Mid-State turn me queer?

No. No, c'mon, Curt. There was that first time, remember? The first time you fucked a guy? You didn't get off on it. I mean, you got off, but you didn't get off. If that makes any sense.

Yeah. Yeah, it does. 'Cause when it happened, it wasn't somethin' I'd exactly planned on. I'd been workin' in the laundry six months when a couple brothers grabbed this fresh meat — not even a kid; a guy in his thirties sent up for embezzlement, I think, but he was white an' the brothers love to nail white guys. They dragged him behind the machines an' this one buck — Shamar? — saw me saw 'em doin' it. He told me if I kept quiet, I could have a turn.

I was still livin' off my right hand, at that time, so I wasn't all that up for it. So I just said, "It's all between you guys."

Shamar smirked an' said, "C'mon, Curt, ain't ya even gonna try it out? I mean, shit, in here it don't mean shit."

"'Cept to the guy who's bein' punked."

"He's ain't no guy, now; he's what you call a commodity."

That hit me as funny. I laughed an' said, "You think if I go back there an' get distracted, you can make me a *commodity*, too?"

"Shit, man," he snarled in a nothin' way, "if I did that, I'd have to kill ya. An' you're white, so it'd be the needle for me. But if I didn't kill ya, I'd have to watch my back the rest of my time in. I seen how you work, how quick you caught on to this place. It's like you was born to it, man, so you'll catch ont' this, soon enough."

"What the fuck's that supposed to mean?"

"Nothin', man. You don't wanna do it, now, that's cool. They's waitin' for me."

He started behind the machines but I stopped him. My last couple of yank sessions hadn't been all that satisfyin', I had to admit, an' now he had my curiosity up.

"Wait, wait...you tellin' me it really helps. Gettin' off like that?"

"Why you think we doin' it?"

"Fuck whitey the only way you can."

His eyes got cold. I got ready for him, just in case. But then he thought about it an' laughed.

"Curt, you got too much fuckin' mouth on you."

"Man, you sound like my mom bitchin' at me."

He laughed even harder then motioned for me to join him.

"C'mon, bro', why don't you try it out? No other way t' know if it's gonna help or not. An' tell you what — I'll even let you pop his cherry."

"I dunno, man..."

"You don't pop it, I will. An' it'd be better for him if you break him in."

"Bullshit, I've seen you in the shower."

"But you ain't seen me in action mode. It ain't how it starts out; it's how it ends up." He swung his hips around, laughin'. "Get it?"

I just rolled my eyes, shook my head, gave it a second more's thought...an' went back there with him.

The guy was face down on the floor in this area that was just a bit wider than the passageway — close to where I took that guard a few years later — an' it was takin' four of the brothers to hold him there. Not so much 'cause he was strong as he was scared. He had good reason to be. These five fuckers'd really do him a number. They'd already pulled his pants an' boxers down to his knees. They must've shoved somethin' in his mouth, because his yellin' was muffled; the machines drowned out what little you could hear.

Shamar slapped me on the back an' said, "Gentlemen, we got a guest. An' as a gracious host, I've offered him first crack at the crack."

The brothers laughed an' one of them smacked the dude's ass, hard. He kept yellin' an' kept strugglin' but it kept doin' him no damn good.

Shamar leaned against the wall, to catch a better view, it looked like. "Use expectorate to lubricate."

"What?" I asked.

"Spit."

"Do this a lot, huh?"

"I gotta answer that?"

I shook my head, unzipped my fly — leavin' the belt nice an' tight, just to be safe — whipped it out an' whipped it up an' helped myself to the offerin'. The guy yelled an' squirmed, but with five men on him, he couldn't do shit.

It wasn't bad, bein' inside him, but I had to put my mind into overdrive to pull Connie into my line of sight. An' it never got past the point of fantasy, y'know? Like I was fuckin' my right hand — no, more like fuckin' a pillow. An' when I was done, I wiped off an' packed away an' shrugged.

"Not bad, but not for me, man."

"It's cool, Curt," said Shamar. "At least you ain't no virgin, no more. Thanks for loosenin' him up for me." Then he showed me his dick an' all I could think was *ouch*.

I went back to work as they got busy. An' I tucked it away as somethin' tried but not my thing. Not till that rich-bitch kid in my cell.

But ya know — an' this is the first time I really put two an' two together — I figure that first fuck may've opened the door to the second one. An' that lead to later ones an' straight to where I was now. I mean, you got a need? You gotta find some way to fill it. Like B follows A an' C follows B. An' maybe you find out what you fill that need with now is better than what you used to fill it with then.

If that makes any sense.

Aw, shit, I was so fuckin' confused. So fucked up. I'd been so busy plannin' this whole operation with Wayne an' fightin' with Connie an' barely makin' a buck an' a half off those dykes I worked for an' thinkin' 'bout what I could do when I got that car an' the cash, I hadn't really thought about what it all meant to me.

This.

What this was doin' to me. But now, in a blindin' flash, I had one of those rare moments where I was able to see just how completely, totally an' absolutely I'd fucked up my life. Startin' with the drugs, goin' through my first rape right up to goin' after Shayes. An' it made me sick to my stomach. I kept tryin' to convince myself that it wasn't too late to stop this train wreck I suddenly saw comin'.

But it was.

It was.

I finished the beer an' popped another. I was startin' to feel a bit better. Physically. An' my mind was easin' back into a blank; that's my safety zone. The beer was beginnin' to give me a buzz — unusual for me after just two.

That's when I remembered I was still wearin' my ski mask, so I whipped it off an' rubbed my face. The little sugar ants were retreatin'. I was finally able to look around an' notice the sky was gettin' cloudy an' a cool wind was pickin' up. Maybe some rain comin' with it. Typical June weather; hot one day, wet as shit the next. But I love the rain. It's clean. Almost makes me feel clean.

I could just hear somethin' fall over inside the shed. Wayne an' Lenny must've already started havin' fun. An' it sounded like the foam was workin' on the walls, since I couldn't really hear anything else above the a/c.

I pushed off from the post an' wandered 'round the yard. I was back to bein' numb. Back to not thinkin'. Back to not feelin' anything about it, one way or the other. I couldn't have gotten my dick up, right then, but I wasn't about to freak, anymore. What's done is done, Curt, ol' buddy; make the best of it.

Then the shed's door blew open an' Shayes came barrelin' out an' slammed headlong into me! We crashed to the little bit of grass an' whipped against the fence, an' suddenly he was screaming, "Police! Help me!" at the top of his lungs!

I acted from instinct. I scrambled on top of him an' rammed my arm against his throat, but he blocked me with his own arms! His wrists were still strapped together but they were in *front* of him! Then he slammed my jaw with his two hands!

We rolled away from the fence an' I grabbed him 'round the chest! He kicked an' tried to flip me away, still screamin' for help, but I had a lock on him, had his arms back to bein' useless! Then Lenny an' Wayne appeared, an' each of them grabbed one of Shaye's legs an' held on with all their might! That gave me a chance to push my way to behind him an' muffle his screams with my left arm as I held his arms tight to his chest with my right, usin' every ounce of strength I had to keep control of him! If his hands hadn't been still tied, he'd have gotten away. We struggled to our feet — Shayes still fightin' like a madman — an' carried him back into the shed.

Through the whole thing, Shayes was screamin', "Lemme go, you fuckin' faggots! Help! Help me! FIRE! FIRE! Faggot! Keep the fuck off me! Motherfuckers! Help! Police!"

The second we were inside, I kicked the door closed, behind me. Then Wayne an' Lenny grabbed some rope an' tied Shayes' ankles back together — at light speed, it seemed. Now that he couldn't kick, they helped me force his arms up over his head an' slip the strap around his wrists into the ring at the end of the cable. Then they pulled the cable up, forcin' him to hang by his wrists. Now he was danglin' off the floor. He could struggle an' curse an' spit as much as he wanted, but he sure as shit wasn't goin' nowhere.

I'd taken most of the beatin' — at least, I got it from the point where Shayes got outside; once things were back under control, I saw Wayne had a cut over his eye an' Lenny had a nosebleed. An' both of 'em were pissed.

"What th' fuck happened?" I asked 'em.

Wayne glared at Lenny an' said, "We were tying his feet to the bed posts, first his left foot and then his right. But Lenny cut the straps around his ankles before I'd secured his left foot. He kicked Lenny and rammed a knee into my back and slipped his hands under his butt before I could do anything to stop him. He yanked off his blindfold and got to the door. I tackled him, but he punched me. Then he ran outside. He was screaming the whole time; didn't you hear him?"

"Not a word," I said. "Shit."

Then I looked at Shayes. He was hangin' from the chain like a side of beef, half his shirt torn away, his shorts 'round his hips, his briefs at an angle. He had curled his arms to pull himself up to try an' free himself from the straps, but they were caught too well inside the ring an' he couldn't get a good hold of the cable to pull himself up higher.

Any questions I had 'bout what we were gonna do vanished. Lookin' back, I can see that's when somethin' else took over. Unstoppable. No barriers. No control. Somethin' I'd only got near to once before, when I lost out on *Chad* an' ripped into the first thing available. The animal in me smelled blood. Smelled its meat. Was lookin' at it an'...lovin' the idea of it. It couldn't of been stopped now if I'd tried. If I'd even wanted to. It was somethin' that just had to happen. An' all that worry an' bullshit I'd been fussin' over went out with the trash. What I needed — deep down needed — meant ten times more to me...no, a thousand times more than anything else I'd ever even thought about. Ever considered. The animal...the lion...the jackal...whatever, it needed to be fed.

Even if it meant prison.

Even if it meant hell.

I grabbed Shayes' ankles an' yanked him down. The straps dug into his wrists an' he cried out. He still tried to kick me, but I had control of him, now. I lifted his legs up, curled my right arm up under them, addin' to the pressure on his wrists. Yeah, they were good legs. Damn good. An' they were mine, now. I let my fingers slip between 'em just above his knees, an' I leaned in real close.

"What th' fuck you think you're pullin', bitch?" I asked, real soft an' low.

Shayes snarled back, "You touch me, motherfucker, I'll fuckin' kill you!"

I chuckled an' smacked his ass with my left hand. "Make up your mind, bitch. I'm a fatherfucker or a motherfucker; I can't be both. Or can I?"

I dropped his legs. He jangled there, gruntin' in pain 'cause of his wrists.

"What'd you get to spread his legs?" I asked Wayne.

He showed me a foot restraint — two soft straps at each

end of a two foot long pole. I took it an' looked it over. The buckles were tarnished an' the leather lips had creases where they'd been used. I smiled an' tightly wrapped one of the straps around Shayes' left ankle, usin' his sock to pad it. He tried to fight me off, but Wayne an' Lenny grabbed his legs an' body to hold him still.

"What the fuck're you think you're gonna do!?" Shayes asked. "You gonna kill me!? You'd better! You fuckin' touch me, you'd fuckin' better fuckin' kill me!"

I just sneered at him an' said to Lenny, "Hold his right leg at the knee."

Lenny did what I said, an' I untied the rope around Shayes' ankles. He tried to kick us away, but he couldn't get the leverage, this time, so I was able to force the leather strap around his right ankle. Now his legs were under control.

"It won't be any good for you, faggot," Shayes said. "I'm gonna fight you the whole time."

Then I went to the cable an' lowered Shayes so he could stand instead of hang. He could barely keep upright, even if he didn't move around so much, so he stood pretty still. He was thinkin' a mile a minute. Tryin' to figure out how he could talk his way out of this. Prayin' he could.

"Listen, man," he said. "I'm not queer. So it won't be any good for you. Listen to me! I'm a *cop*. If — if you do this to me — any of you — an' if — if you do kill me, it's a capital offense. My buddies'll come lookin' for you. They'll *find* you! And it's the needle! For *all* of you! Can't you see how dumb that is?"

In answer, I just stepped back an' opened my arms, sayin' to Lenny an' Wayne, "You boys wanna do the honors?"

Wayne chuckled, grabbed Shayes' ratty shirt an' ripped it open. He shredded it in stages, first away from his chest an' then off his shoulders. Strip by strip. Takin' his time as Lenny focused the camera in on 'em. Probably tight on every thread of cotton as it ripped away. I just stood there an' watched, feelin' fire spread from my crotch through my legs an' my gut an' my chest an' my arms down to my fingers an' up to my throat an' face as

Shayes' upper body was made bare, before me. It was almost like some — some ritual sacrifice in its feel. An' I loved it.

Shayes gulped then fought to keep control of his breathin' as Wayne ran his hands over his pecs. I nudged Wayne, motioned for him to get behind Shayes. He did. But slipped his arms 'round the guy's body an' kept playin' with his tits, makin' him squirm.

I looked Shayes over from head to toe. Yeah, his abs were just like a guy'd want — solid but not stupidly so. With good pecs toppin' 'em off. Hair fannin' over tanned skin. No way was I gonna think of him as anything but a guy, but that didn't bug me, anymore.

It's funny — I felt pissed at how perfect he looked. An' how easy it was for him. But at the same time, I felt *joy* at how perfect he looked. How real. An' all of it was without a second of confusion. This was how it was gonna be — maybe how it was supposed to be. I dunno. It all felt a bit unreal. I had to touch the hair on his chest — play with it — just to make sure it wasn't some figment of my imagination. He tried to twist away from my hands.

"No! No, this is rape," he choked out. "This is kidnapping. Of a cop. That's a Federal offense. Fuckin' *federal*! Please — please, think about what you're doing."

I walked around him, nudgin' Wayne out of the way so I could get a clear view. Wayne stood aside, watchin' me with that spooky look of his, but I didn't care. I was focused on Shayes.

His ass was full, but not really what you'd call a bubble butt. An' man, even spread apart, his legs looked good. Nice form to 'em, even with his shorts droopin' over his hips. In fact, the way the elastic to his briefs sort of rolled across the top of his ass, showin' a hint of a tan line, it really got my dick to stirin'. I wanted to see his tightie-whities. So I stepped back an' nodded to Wayne.

"Shorts."

Wayne grabbed his baggy shorts an' tore at them. Shayes cried out as they shredded away in strips an' threads. First one leg then the other. The zipper gave way last. An' then he was standin' there — arms strung up above his head; legs spread apart by the restraints; a blindin' pair of white briefs his only cover...

An' I wanted him like I've never wanted anything before.

I knew — didn't really see it but knew — Lenny'd taken a camera off its tripod an' was focused on me. I snickered an' traced my right hand down Shayes' back, from the edge of his hair to the top of his ass. He felt cold. Shivery. Wet from sweatin'. He felt like electricity.

I unzipped my jeans an' let my dick out. I was hard, but not so very much so. Not till I slipped up behind him an' let it push against the white cotton that covered his ass; then it got to poundin'. He jolted an' tried to squirm away, but I wrapped my arms around his waist an' held him close.

Oh, shit. Holy shit. I was ownin' him. My heart felt ready to bust, it felt so nice to mold myself against him like that. Feel him shiverin'. Taste his sweat. Smell his hair. Oh, shit, he was all mine. An' I was ownin' him.

"Oh, no," he said, "please. Please. You can't do this to me. I've never done anything like it. Never."

I let my dick glide between his legs an' push up against the back of his balls. He was breathless. Shiverin' even harder in my arms. I could feel his heart poundin' next to mine. I nestled my face into the curve of his right shoulder — where it meets his neck — an' I whispered to him, "I can do anything I fuckin' want."

"No! No..."

"No?" I worked my dick back an' forth between his legs, rubbin' up against the soft white cotton. Bumpin' its head against his balls. He clenched his muscles an' tried to avoid me, but he couldn't. "That's what's gonna be inside you, soon."

"Motherfucker — no!"

"If you fight me, it'll hurt more. But if you're nice, I can make it easy. But tell you what — I'll let you show us how nice you can be. Show us you're worth bein' easy with. Before I fuck you, I'll let you suck off my buddy."

"I'll fuckin' bite it off!"

I reached around, grabbed his tits an' twisted 'em, pulled at 'em till he cried out in pain.

"I'm the one in control, here. You're gonna suck him off. An' make him happy. Which means, careful with the teeth. 'Cause if you do bite him, I'll cut your balls off."

"You're gonna fuckin' kill me, anyway! I won't let a guy's dick in my — "

I twisted his tits, again, then whispered, "It ain't just about you, asshole."

"What?!"

"It's more than just you here."

"What — what d'you mean?"

I smiled an' nibbled at his ear, an' then I whispered, "I know where you live."

He froze. Then he looked 'round at me, confused...but not totally.

"You got a nice family," I added, with just a hint of a smile. "We could keep you here for days. Weeks. Till the uproar dies down. An' I could come an' go as I pleased. Go wherever I pleased."

He went white. I knew I didn't have to say another word, but I wanted Wayne an' Lenny to know it was all right.

"You gonna play nice, now?"

He hesitated...then looked away from me. An' stopped tryin' to keep away from my dick. An' when I let my hands trail away from his tits an' down his stomach, an' I slipped them under the elastic to his briefs, an' I ran my fingers over his pubes an' around his dick, an' I found the "Y" front to his briefs an' gripped that an' ripped 'em to shreds, he barely flinched.

I stepped back to look him over, again. An' still liked what I saw. His butt was smooth an' hair fanned over it, but not too much. An' yeah, he had a tan line, but a squarish one, like what you get from swimming trunks. An' his back was formed good an' everything fit together just right. I couldn't help it, I had to run my hands over him. Over every square inch of his body. Just to make sure he was really there.

So I did.

He let me.

Didn't squirm, too much. Just let out little whimpers, now an' then. It's crazy. I'd done this to girls, before. Shit, Connie loved it. Slow fingers just barely touchin' skin, drifitn' up an' down an' around. It'd drive her nuts. Drive any girl I was with nuts. An' send bolts of lightnin' up my arms to my brain. I loved it as much as them, but I'd never — never even thought about doin' this to a guy. But here I was — doin' it an'...an' startin' to feel drunk from it.

Finally, I couldn't take any more. I stepped back an' pulled off my jeans an' shirt, removed my socks an', finally, slipped my briefs down my legs. I stepped out of them an' walked around to face Shayes. He was breathin' hard. Not from fear, now. No. I could see how his tits were pointed. An' his dick was more full. Not hard. Not even really gettin' there, yet. But startin'. I could tell. I stroked it a little. Just to show him I could.

He wouldn't look at me. Refused to, till I pressed myself against him — lettin' my hard dick crush against his softer one — an' wrapped my arms 'round him. Then he glanced at me, sideways.

"We got an understandin'?" I whispered.

He just looked away, again. Meanin', *Yes*.

I put one arm around his waist an' lifted him up, then reached up with the other, worked the plastic straps through the opening in the ring an' let his arms drop around my neck. I smiled at him. He just licked his lips, shiverin'.

I slipped my free hand down his back, brushed it over his butt an' wound up inside his left thigh, my other arm stayin' 'round his torso. I lifted him up an' carried him to the bed, like a bride. I lay him on it, face up, an' knelt back to look him over. His wrists were red an' cut an' beginnin' to swell from the plastic strap. I motioned to Wayne, who handed me a blade. An' I slit the strap away. I guided his hands to the leather straps attached to the head posts' dowel an' wrapped 'em 'round his wrists. Then, last but not least, I took off the restraints on his legs.

He lay there, arms bound above his head, legs still spread apart, shiverin' not from cold but from anticipation. From fear. His dick lay to the left, still more limp than not, but now it had a slopin' form to it that looked, I dunno, right. He didn't try to hide himself; he just looked at the ceilin'.

Wayne stepped closer to the bed an' whispered, "He's beautiful. Everything about him is."

I turned to Wayne an' said, "Have at it."

In a nano-second, Wayne was on the bed, naked. He looked at me, waitin' for me to give him a sign, so I nodded. Then he put his dick to Shayes' mouth. The guy crushed his lips closed an' turned away. Wouldn't open up. Not till I squeezed his balls with my hand an' whispered, "C'mon, buddy, prove you're worth it."

The guy gave me a look so full of hate, if it'd been a knife, I'd of been sliced to ribbons. Then he swallowed an' slowly let his lips part an' Wayne slipped inside. Shoved in deep. Shayes gagged, but after a moment, he started workin' on it. Nothin' great about this blowjob, from what I could see, but fuckin' Wayne didn't care. Fact is, it only took him a minute to let loose. Took both him an' Shayes by surprise.

Shayes choked an' coughed an' spit the dick out, gaggin' from Wayne's crap. One last spurt hit him on the chin, then Wayne leaned back, breathin' deep an' happy. All he could say, over an' over, was, "Oh, shit. Oh, shit."

I leaned over to whisper into Wayne's ear, "No teeth marks?"

Wayne shook his head, barely able to croak out, "It was perfect. Perfect." His eyes were tearin' up.

"An' quick," I sneered.

"To start," Wayne sneered back.

I nodded an' moved to between Shayes' legs. I lifted them up an' positioned myself to where his ass was restin' on my thighs an' my dick was bumpin' on top his balls. His legs were propped up on my shoulders. He didn't like it — tried to shift away — but I grabbed his ass to hold him in place. He stopped squirmin'. I took a jar of Vaseline from beside the bed an' scooped some out on my finger. An' I slipped it between the cheeks of his ass an' smeared it 'round his hole. He gulped an' grimaced but said nothin'. Then I lubed some onto my dick, found his hole with my finger an' pressed the head of my dick against it.

"Wait," he whispered, his voice shakin'. "Will — will you at least use a condom?"

Fuckin' idiot. Like I got AIDS? In answer, I began pushin' my way into him. Slow, like I promised.

He clenched tight, automatically, an' grimaced. But the Vaseline did its job an' I slipped inside. Slowly glided in deeper an' deeper till I could feel his balls touching my pubes. He was gaspin' an' tryin' hard not to cry out, but little yelps of pain kept escapin'. Once I was all the way in, I held still an' looked at him.

Oh, holy fuckin' Jesus, I didn't want to move. At that moment, havin' his ass wrapped around my dick, flexin' an' pushin' at it like he was — I felt this...this instant of peace. Felt a moment of perfection. It was like, this was all I'd ever wanted to do. This was just how it was supposed to be. I owned the world an' the moon an' the stars. I rivaled God in my power an' control. An' I never wanted it to end.

But then I started pumpin' inside him. An' it got even better than I could ever have imagined.

I took it slow with Shayes. Nothin' to rush. No reason to prove I was top dog. He already knew that. Everybody did. No, this time I was out for me. This time it was just sex. Slidin' in, my dick sent a rush down to my balls that was as good as the first time you snort coke. Pullin' back made my thighs quiver an' burn an' tingle with feelin's I never knew were possible. Every little whimper or moan he let escape sent my brain reelin'. Even the hair on his legs ticklin' my skin an' even my tits doubled every second of pleasure I got from bein' inside him.

Oh, shit, shit, shit, this was nothin' like bein' with Connie.

I leaned in an' began suckin' on his tits. First one, then the other. The hair around 'em felt soft, like down, an' teased my nose an' lips an' tongue as I played with the brown knob. His pecs were hard — not soft like a chick's breasts or even Carter's — an' pressed back against my chin when I brushed against them.

He gasped at me, "Please, don't...do...that."

I sucked on 'em, harder. I cupped his ass in my hands, playin' with the bit of hair that danced across it. It was full an' firm — not flat or soft like a chick's ass or hard like my first punk's — an' fit my hands perfectly. I loved playin' with it almost as much as he hated me doin' it.

Slow in.

Slow out.

No rush. Not today.

Enjoy.

I straightened up an' ran my hands up his legs to curl in around his thighs. The hair was a bit coarser but still felt fine, an' it tickled my wrists as I pumped. I was dizzy from the feel of it.

"C'mon...man," Shayes grunted, "today, okay? Get it...get it over with...will ya?"

I withdrew almost all the way then pushed back in, even more slowly than before. *Fuck him,* was the first thought in my mind, an' I almost let go with a chuckle that welled up deep inside me. Sometimes I crack myself up. An' that almost brought out another laugh.

I looked down at his dick an' saw it finally startin' to really stir. I think for the first time in my life, I actually considered another man's dick as somethin' worth appreciatin'. An' as dicks go, Shayes had a nice one. It wasn't as round as mine. More like a little oval. But the skin around the shaft was smooth an' clean an' the head — the helmet, my mom called it the one or two times she bathed me; what a weird fuckin' thing to remember at a time like this — that was just as smooth an' a soft pink. My head gets to be huge — almost too big in proportion to my shaft

— but his looked like it might be just the right size. Looked like I was about to find out.

Little faster. Little faster. Not much, though. Don't want this to end too soon. Just a little longer.

Shayes hadn't noticed he was gettin' a hard-on but Lenny sure had. He was watchin' from the side of the bed, his camera back on its tripod. It an' his eyes were glued to the guy's dick. I watched him watch it grow bigger an' bigger till it was floppin' around on his gut. It wasn't gonna be anywhere near as big as mine but Lenny didn't care.

Shayes finally realized he was hard an' looked down at his dick, stunned. "What th' fuck?"

I snickered, "Never done this before, huh? Right."

Shayes shook his head, "No, man — what're you doin' to me? What th' fuck — ?"

I shoved deep into him, harder than I had before. He cried out an' looked away from me, his breathin' gettin' faster an' faster. His dick was still hard though not quite primed yet. So I looked at Lenny an' nodded for him to go for it.

Lenny carefully slipped onto the bed — out of the way of his camera — an' slowly reached over an' touched Shayes' dick. The guy jolted an' tried to wiggle away, but I'd already dug my fingers into his thighs an' had a good lock on his legs. He couldn't do a fuckin' thing I didn't want him to do.

"No, don't...don't!"

Lenny looked at me an' I smiled, "Go ahead."

He took Shayes' dick in one hand an' began to stroke it. He used his other hand to caress the top of Shayes' balls.

The guy started to freak, screamin', "No! No! Don't!"

I started pumpin' into him, faster, deeper, my own breathin' gettin' to be as fast as his. Lenny kept milkin' him for all he was worth. Then he leaned down an' licked Shayes' shaft. Shayes tensed up, tighter than I've ever felt any of my punks do, an' his ass squeezed hard against my dick an' I almost shot my wad, right there. But I held on. Barely. An' I kept pumpin'.

Finally, Shayes' dick was about as hard as it was gonna get.

An' I felt Lenny's head down there, suckin' on it. Shayes' cried out an' started hollerin'. Didn't do a damn bit of good for him. I was still rammin' him an' Lenny was still suckin' on him an' he was still tied to the bed an' his legs were still caught in my grip. An' finally, after maybe ten minutes of us workin' on him, all he could do was let it rip!

He jolted. Almost pulled himself off me an' *did* yank his dick from Lenny's mouth. An' then he started to fire! I mean, he splashed shit all across Lenny's face an' onto his own gut. Some of it whipped up to land on my chest an' it seemed to go everywhere. I just held on, but then his ass slid back down on my dick an' he gripped me so hard, I couldn't hold back anymore. I plowed deeper into him an' let go. Let go until my balls ached from the spasms.

What's wild is, I was so lost in the whole crash of — of feelin's an' emotions an' fireworks an' all, I didn't know when Wayne an' Lenny pulled me back by my hips to let my dick slide out of Shayes so the camera could catch it spewin' all over the guy. All I know for sure is — when I was finally done, I collapsed on top of Shayes an' curled my arms around him an' ground my dick against his in a way that seemed like religion.

An' then...an' then I kissed him.

On the lips.

Full an' complete an' gentle an' without hesitation. My mouth seemed to mold into his, an' I tasted somethin' salty an' moist. Maybe my cum, maybe his, maybe just the sweat on his skin.

An' I...I think — I'd almost swear — no, I'm sure...abso-fuckin'-lutely sure...he kissed me back.

An' somethin' behind my heart gave a leap.

An' I almost started to cry from it.

Then I drifted away, wishin' I could stay there with him, forever.

Chapter Seven

I had this dream while I was out — I think it was a dream. I think it was. Anyway, I was flyin' through the sky, all in my prison clothes, on my back with my first girl. The first girl I slept with — what's her name — Ramona. Yeah, Ramona Verdugo on top of me.

Shit, ol' Ramona. I hadn't thought about her in years. Golden skin. Raven hair. Eyes so brown they looked black. An' tits? Oh, man, she put melons to shame. Fuckin' Ramona. We were hot an' heavy in high school — her a junior, me a freshman. Didn't make sense, but we collided in a hallway one day like a couple cars on the 101 an' stayed stuck to each other till fuckin' Anthony got me busted.

Anyway, our first time together was up on Zuma Beach, north of Malibu. Her old man had this primo '57 Dodge Coronet convertible. Red with white trim an' interior. Little fins on the tail. Looked like it was flyin' even when it was sittin' still, an' nobody was allowed to drive it but him. Threat of death kind of shit, y'know. So this one day early in spring, we cut class an' she palmed the extra set of keys she wasn't supposed to know about, an' I drove us down the Ten an' up PCH. It's funny — fifteen years old an' I already knew how to drive, smoke an' drink football players under the table. An' I had that nice little business goin' in the *weed* department at school, so I always had money. Yeah, I had my mom an' her fuckin' husband tryin' to lay claim to some control over me, but that wasn't goin' anywhere. So all in all, life was good.

God, that Dodge could go. Even with its too-cool push-button automatic. It had a V-eight with power enough to snap your neck if you hit the gas too hard. An' drivin' it that first time, glidin' up the coast on a perfect California day, Ramona beside me, her left hand in my crotch workin' me up, my right hand around her shoulders an' strokin' one of her tits — I was fuckin' king of the world.

We played on the beach, the rest of the day, then grabbed some sandwiches from a grocery store close by an' talked this stoned surfer into buyin' us a six pack. He brought us fuckin' Miller Lite for Christ's sake. An' when we were done eatin' an' it was dark, we put up the top an' got busy in the back seat.

Damn, that thing was so wide, you could stretch out on it. I mean, I could then; I was still growin'. An' Ramona, she's small for the size of her tits. So we got all hot an' heavy, kissin' an' touchin' an' grabbin' — she liked to grab my ass, for some reason — then we whipped a blanket over us an' I unzipped an' popped out an' slipped inside her without a thought. Shit, I'd seem my mom fuckin' guys so many times, I knew exactly what to do. I remember bein' impressed — not surprised or happy or freaked out — at how nice it felt before I went at it.

As we got close to the finish line, Ramona circled her legs around mine an' grabbed my ass an' pulled me harder against her. I came first...lots sooner than I do now...so she kept pullin' me against her till she was done. Then she bit my left tit. Drew blood.

I yelped an' yanked away from her an' said, "What the fuck?!"

She just chuckled, licked her lips an' kissed my other tit. Then she said, "That makes you mine."

I laughed, an' we went at it, again.

Like I said, we were together till I was sent to County. Even her dad raisin' all kinds of shit about us takin' the car didn't mean jack; we'd sneak it off anytime we wanted, since I'd been sharp enough to get an extra set of keys made. Oh, I'd try to park it exactly like he parked it, so he wouldn't notice. But sometimes I was just a little too out of it to give a fuck. We laughed our asses off about it — till he sold the damn thing.

But then she heard about me an' Paco an' his vatos. Seems this cousin of hers was in for shopliftin' an' got the skinny from one of the guards in exchange for a couple tabs of acid. When she found out, she stopped talkin' to me. Wouldn't answer the phone. Wouldn't even come to the door when I went to her place. Only clue I got she knew was the last time I was there; her dad smirked at me an' muttered, "Maricon," an' she told me she didn't want to go out that day 'cause she had a headache. So I went out an' asked a vato buddy of mine what that word meant — maricon. An' he fuckin' told me. Fuckin' Ramona fuckin' dumped me 'cause I got fucked.

Fuckin' bitch.

So I shifted to the club scene, where only a couple people knew me, an' built up a new rep till I finally collided with Connie. An' I put that cunt out of my mind. Till this dream.

Like I said, I was flyin' on my back, in my prison grey. Her on top of me, straddlin' me, which she never did 'cause then she couldn't dig her nails into my butt. She was tearin' at my shirt with her hands an' teeth an' screamin', "C'mon, you fuckin' pussy, giddy up, giddy up!" But my shirt wouldn't tear. Buttons wouldn't come undone. I had a ragin' hard-on in my pants but the fuckin' zipper was locked in place. So she slapped me. Fuckin' hard. An' it fuckin' hurt. I thought you weren't supposed to feel pain in dreams. Then all of a sudden, it was Connie on top me an' Ramona was under me, tearin' at my ass through my pants. She was usin' her teeth. Didn't work. Connie had her scissors an' was tryin' to cut the uniform away, but they broke. An' Connie started to cry.

Then Ramona dropped away an' Connie an' I flipped to where I was on top her an' she froze into a statue. That's when I saw we were miles above the earth an' we weren't flyin', we were fallin'. An' somebody was on top me, tearin' my shirt away like it was paper. Then tearin' my pants down like they were nothin'. I thought it was Ramona, again, but it was Father Tello. Which didn't make sense; he'd never tried to pull any shit with me. But now he we was feelin' me up rough, grabbin' an' pokin' an' pinchin' an' proddin' an' whisperin', "If only you'd let me. If only you'd let me."

Then Tello an' Connie were gone an' I was lyin' on top one of that Dodge's tail fins an' I was still fallin'. But now Wayne was standin' in front of me, naked an' slappin' me an' the ground was rushin' up to me and then suddenly I was on it, but I hadn't landed. I was just...there. Finally I looked 'round an' the world began to change shape around me. Into that room.

Where I'd just fucked Shayes.

But I wasn't where I was supposed to be, in there. I remembered I was lyin' on top Shayes when I drifted, but now I was off the bed an' lookin' at the floor but I wasn't lyin' on it. Which didn't make any sense.

That's when I realized I was lyin' on some kind of post with my arms droopin' down the sides, so I tried to sit up but I couldn't move my hands. I yanked at 'em an' saw I was caught in the handcuffs attached to that hook in the floor! My legs were caught, too!

What the fuck?

Man, I snapped awake then. I looked around an' saw I was on that leather-covered sawhorse. Lengthwise, not bent over it. My feet were chained to the legs, exposin' my butt to the world. But I felt like I was covered, somehow. I looked around an' saw I was back in my briefs. I didn't get it. When'd I put them back on?

I heard somebody gruntin' to my left.

I looked over an' saw Shayes tied to the chair by this wild system of ropes an' knots that made him look like some macramé project. Shreds of some old clothes — not his — hung from his shoulders an' waist, like he'd been dressed an' stripped, again. An' he was squirmin' as if he's in pain. Which he probably was; there were some wires attached to his dick an' looked like to his balls, too. Some kind of transformer was givin' off a soft hum under the chair an' Lenny — naked as fuck with a ragin' hard-on — was playin' rough with the guy. Two of the video cameras sat on tripods, tapin' it all.

"It really works, Wayne," Lenny chuckled. "I can feel the current. Just touching his tits — " he touched 'em with his dick, the sick fuck " — gives me a little shock. And look how he loves it."

Which was bullshit. Even as fuzzy as I was, I could tell Shayes was out of it. His eyes were rolled back an' his lids were flutterin' an' all he could do was twist an' moan.

Shit, how long had I been out?

Lenny kept runnin' his hands all over Shayes, gigglin' like some crazy clown, twisin' an' slappin' an' pinchin' in ways that even hurt to watch. The guy just groaned. His breathin' was harsh. Lenny snickered, "He's about to cum, Wayne."

I heard Wayne's voice say, "Good."

An' then he did. Not huge, like with me. Just a little. But enough for Lenny.

Shayes' head rolled forward, like he was passin' out, so that skinny fuck turned off the transformer, shifted the cameras around, grabbed Shayes' hair an' yanked his head back. He slapped the guy, twice, then leaned in close.

"Now be nice or else," Lenny said, then he pulled Shayes' mouth open an' slipped his dick inside. Shayes didn't fight him. Didn't do anything at all. Probably couldn't. But Lenny still acted like he was forcin' him. An' he was happy.

I started feelin' sick to my stomach, seein' it. I helped these fuckin' perverts? Shit, how fuckin' low had I gone?

Then Wayne piped in, "Don't take too long, Lenny."

That's when I felt hands on my butt. I looked around...an', of course, fuckin' Wayne was a naked as fuckin' Lenny an' just as fuckin' ready to do business.

"Fuckin' shit, Wayne," I snarled, "what the fuck's this all about?!"

"Oh, just fulfilling a fantasy of mine," he said in this half-tone voice. "Raping two beautiful men at one time."

"If you think you're gonna fuck me, cocksucker — !"

"Cut it out, Curt," he sneered back. "I know your cherry is

long since gone. So why're you so protective of it?"

Then he whipped his hand across my tail, hard as shit! I jolted at how much it hurt. Didn't know the fat fucker was that strong. "I've sucked your cock enough, you little tease. I've paid for your ass a dozen times. Now I'm going to get *my* money's worth."

He tore my briefs off me, in shreds. I flinched at how it felt. Then I noticed the third camera was catchin' it all. In seconds, all that was left was the elastic 'round my waist. He snapped at it a couple times, but didn't really try to get rid of it. Then he pressed his dick between my ass cheeks.

"Oh, yes, baby," he whispered. "I've wanted you like this from the second I saw you."

"What the fuck, Wayne — why're you pullin' this shit on me?! You got what you wanted!"

"No, *you* got what you wanted. You wanted to fuck up Officer Shayes — I could see that from the second he called you a faggot — and from the looks of things, you did a damned good job on him. I'd say he's in shock."

"'Cause of the shit you pulled on him while I was out. How many times you sent a guy into it, before?"

"Curt, please. I've never gone this far, before. Never had to. There are plenty of young men in the world willing to do — oh, just about anything for the right amount of money. So long as they don't know they're being videotaped. Or exactly how far I intend to — shall we say, *take things*."

"Until they're primed and ready and then hear in detail what you want to do," Lenny chimed in, breathless.

"Hurry up, Lenny. Sleeping beauty's awake and I want all three cameras to catch every moment of this."

I looked around to catch Lenny pullin' out an' shootin' on Shayes' face. Then he let Shayes' head drop back to his chest an' looked at me. I got real cold when I saw the smile on his face. He didn't look so scared...so mousy, anymore; he looked like a cat that just finished off a sparrow.

"Gimme a minute," he whispered, "we can do this, again."

"No rush, honey," said Wayne, still rubbin' his dick against my ass. "We got all night. I popped some Viagra." Then he moved around in front of me, sayin', "You're the first one I wanted to get like this, no matter what, Curt. Mainly because of how sure you were that I could be played like some desperate queen seeking cock at any price. You see, I'd already heard about you from some friends of mine. Men like myself who told me all about your, *Okay, you can suck me off for the right amount* attitude."

"I'm the one who recognized you when you came in," said Lenny as he swallowed some pills. Probably somethin' to get him hot an' horny, again. I hoped it gave him a fuckin' heart attack. "That's why I bought you a beer so quickly. And add to that the discussion turning to whether or not any man could be made to cum — well, I just had to prove to you that I knew it was true, even for you. Especially for you."

"What you goin' on about?"

"I *have* done it, Curt. That boy in Texas, he *wasn't* even the first. Of course, I usually had to use more artificial means than you; I'm not as well endowed. But that's what toys are for. After all, whatever works, which I tested out on a couple of guys who became too frightened to keep it up during playtime. Haven't been disappointed, yet. But you? You were a challenge. You're too strong to overpower. And too crafty to fall for the *Let me tie you up, just a little* line. And I quickly saw I'd never be able to get you drunk enough or access to your beer long enough to slip something in it. But when Lenny popped up with that little bet and you took him up on it, that's when I knew how to get you right where I wanted you."

"I knew he was a cop," said Lenny as he shifted the cameras. "He busted a friend of mine, six months ago. And very legitimately. My pal answered the door with an erection in his hand. Young Officer Shayes didn't bat an eye; he just pulled out his badge and took him downtown. In his robe."

Wayne chuckled as his hands kneaded my back. "He whined about it over drinks a few days later. Told us everything.

Even the number he called. It was too beautiful to pass up."

"You tellin' me this whole fuckin' thing was a set-up!?"

"From the moment we left the bar."

"That's bullshit. Lenny was fuckin' scared shitless when Shayes pulled his badge!"

"He's an actor, Curt. I told you, remember?"

"You should see me do *MacBeth* in the park, sometime."

"I mentioned it just to see if you'd caught on. Like a typical jerk focused on his dick, you hadn't."

"But — but, Wayne, you didn't want us to go for it! An' — an' when you came out to help back Shayes down — an' — an' after — after..."

I wanted to keep callin' on his bullshit, but I was finally startin' to see it wasn't just bullshit. How Wayne *let* Lenny plan things, at first. How easy he was comin' in to back me up against Shayes. How smooth everything'd gone from that point. An' the bells goin' off in my head an' the voice warnin' me things wasn't right, somehow. Shit, I didn't want to believe it but I knew the fucker was layin' it out for me — me bein' on this fuckin' sawhorse was the whole point of the whole fuckin' mess. An' I felt like such a fuckin' idiot.

"You played your part ten times better than I expected, Curt," Wayne said, then he moved back behind me an' lay on top of me, put his head against my shoulder an' motioned to Shayes. "And having this man was so much more beautiful than I could ever have imagined. It was perfect. Such a pity."

Now I may be a fuckin' idiot, but I ain't so dumb that I couldn't figure out what Wayne meant. Shayes saw us. Saw our faces. He wasn't supposed to, but he did. An' he saw where he was. The back yard, anyway. If we let him go, he might do nothin'. Especially since we'd videotaped him suckin' a guy off an' shootin' a load while bein' butt-fucked. But he might also file a report. An' he could I-D us. I-D me, for sure, since I had a record. Me, I'd already figured that out, but since I had a better idea of how suspicious an' full of shit cops are an' how macho they always *have* to seem to each other, I was open to takin' the chance. We could do the *his word against mine* thing, again. But Lenny an' Wayne, they had too much to lose — their home, their freedom, maybe their reputations, even each other. An' that was too chancy for them to ignore. They'd have to kill him. I'd thought about them tryin' to do that an' how I'd handle it, but I didn't think they'd be dumb enough to think they could do it to me, too.

Wayne leaned back an' I heard him pop the top to the Vaseline. A second later, he was probin' me with a glob of it. I couldn't move enough to squirm; they'd made sure the cuffs were holdin' me too tight an' strapped a belt across my waist to hold me to the horse. That's when I started losin' it. Started flashin' back to when Paco'd fucked me. But I knew it wasn't gonna do me any good to freak, so I pulled a Shayes.

"Wayne, you fuckin' idiot, this fuckin' cop ain't worth the needle. An' trust me, man — if you kill him, they'll find you. He's got your sperm in his gut, man. Think about it!"

Wayne pulled my butt open an' probed me with his thumbs. "But they have to find him, first. And that's what the Angeles National Forest is for. It gives you someplace to bury a body. Nice and deep!"

An' he slammed inside me.

An' I fuckin' screamed, I have t' admit it.

He wanted me to. An' I tried not to. But it exploded out of me! Then he slipped the bandana 'round my neck an' began to twist it tight.

"I won't be so quick, this time," he muttered as he pumped in an' out of me an' slowly twisted the bandana tighter an' tighter. An' I felt Lenny start to play with me, down below. Play rough.

Motherfuckin' son-of-a-bitch, I wasn't fuckin' gonna die like this! Not bein' strangled while I'm bein' butt-fucked by some fat-assed faggot. No fuckin' way!

I made myself stay in control. Even as the bandana got tighter. An' I looked at the handcuffs. An' all but laughed. They were the same cheap-assed things they'd shown me, before, wrapped around a metal dowl between the legs. I yanked at 'em. They didn't give. I yanked, again. No go.

Wayne was pumpin' harder into me. An' it was fuckin' rippin' me apart! I didn't think his dick was that big! He kept mutterin', "Oh, perfect. Oh, perfect." Over an' over an' over an' I wanted to fuckin' smash his fuckin' face in just for sayin' that. An' at the same time, Lenny was gettin' rougher an' rougher. It felt like he was tryin' to tear my dick off. I kept lettin' loose with grunts of pain, too, no matter what I did. It fuckin' pissed me off, even more.

I was beginnin' to gasp for air, the bandana was so tight. I started seein' spots in front of my eyes. My head was poundin' like it wanted to drop off. An' then my dick started to get hard! It freaked me! I'd heard about guys who choke themselves to get an erection, but I didn't know it'd work like this! I strained harder at the cuffs.

I heard Lenny gigglin' from underneath me, "Careful, careful, save some for me."

Wayne was pumpin' faster, now. He was probably 'bout ready to cum — only good thing about this was, he's a fast shooter — an' that really fuckin' pissed me off. Motherfucker. He was gonna bury both me an' Shayes in the fuckin' ground, both of us full of his an' Lenny's shit an' probably lay us there just like we were, earlier! Shit, that fuckin' made me blind pissed off! I wasn't fuckin' gonna let him!

An' then he was firin' his load inside me. I could feel it. I didn't feel anything like that when Paco did it, an' it freaked me out so much that when I yanked at the handcuffs, this time, they snapped! I slammed my elbow back against Wayne's fuckin' face, sending him flyin' off me, an' the horse toppled over with me still on it, crashin' onto Lenny!

Damn, that fuckin' thing was heavy. It nearly crushed my leg. But it also bent one of the loops holdin' my ankle straps so I could get one leg free. I set to gettin' the belt 'round my waits undone so I could reach the other ankle.

I wasn't worried about Wayne; he was out, cold. But I

realized Lenny'd got free an' was scramblin' to his feet. I was just able to reach him. I grabbed him by a leg an' tripped him. Then I dragged him back to me. I almost had a good hold of him when he kicked me in the chest an' I let go.

He bolted to his feet an' grabbed the knife an' jumped at me! He tried to shove it into my back, but I was able to twist around just enough to where it only sliced my side. An' then I had hold of him. Had my arm around his neck. An' he was screamin' an' fightin' as I grabbed the hand that held the knife an' turned it around an' pushed it into his skinny, hairless chest! Blood spewed everywhere as he screamed an' stopped fightin'. I shoved him off me.

I grunted an' kicked an' pulled at the loop where my leg was still cuffed till I snapped it off, then I found the buckle to the belt an' ripped it open. The cuffs were still 'round my wrists an' ankles, but I was free. I stumbled back, blood glidin' from the cut in my side.

Everything was white around me. Couldn't see a fuckin' thing very clear. All I could hear was Wayne moanin' an' Lenny wheezin' an' gaspin' an' cryin' an' sayin', "Doctor. Please, doctor." He may've even gurgled a little. Guess I cut a lung.

I stumbled around in this...this white fog. Somehow wound up outside. An' it seemed just as dark an' white, out there. I found the van, more by touch than anything. Found Shayes' pistol an' found my way back into the shed.

An' I emptied it into the two fucks.

I heard both of 'em screamin'.

Motherfuckers. Try an' fuck with me, you'll find out what kind of deep shit you got yourself into.

I dunno how long I stumbled 'round there. Butt naked. Crazy as shit. Mutterin' over their bodies. Must've been hours. Probably minutes. What jumped me out of it was I fell over Shayes. Landed hard. Tasted blood in my mouth. I looked 'round an' saw one of my legs was restin' on him. He was lyin' on his side, still tied to the chair. I scrambled around to him an' gently untied him. Took forever, there were so many knots. Then I picked him up — don't know how I found the strength — an' lay him back on the bed. Tended to him like I would my brother. Brushed back his hair an' checked his face. Put my hand over his heart an' felt relief that it was still beatin'. Not strong but definitely beatin'.

A fresh wave of hate rushed over me. Bastards hurt him. Probably tortured him. Motherfuckers were gonna kill him an' he was mine, not theirs! Motherfuckers! He was *mine*! I stumbled over to their bodies an' kicked 'em both. Over an' over an' over till I collapsed on the floor, sobbin'.

I dunno how long I lay there, but it finally struck me that it was dark, outside. Completely dark. Which meant it was after nine. I must've been out three or four hours, at least. But how? Why? Unless...there was somethin' in those beers I drank. I'd started feelin' better once they were in me. Feelin' — shit, feelin' too good about it. About what I was doin'. Could that've been why? The tops came off those bottles really easy. So they'd planned to put me out an' have Shayes all to themselves? Shit, what'd they do to him while I wasn't here?

I looked him over, careful. Gentle. There were bruises an' marks all over. Cuts around his tits. Slime all over his face an' chest. His hair was matted from it. He had burns where those wires'd been. An' on the inside of his legs. Jesus Christ, they HAD fuckin' tortured him.

I got up an' kicked both their fuckin' bodies, again. Kicked 'em over an' over like they could still feel it. Fuckin' hurt my foot — broke a toe, I found out — an' crashed back on the bed, beside Shayes. I lay there for a minute, lookin' at the foam chunks coverin' the ceilin' an' feelin' like I wanted to cry. But I couldn't; Shayes' skin was feelin' cold.

I looked around for a blanket but couldn't find anything, so I wrapped him in the sheet that was on the bed. It was bloody, but it worked okay. Then I tore that fuckin' room apart till I found a set of keys to the cuffs 'round my hands an' wrists, an' I got them off me. Then I realized I was feelin' cold, too. An' remembered I was still butt-fuckin' naked. Standin' in front of two dead men sloshed in blood. An' one of 'em was still lookin' at me. Wayne. His eyes were open an' his mouth was almost in a sneer, like he was mockin' me.

Oh, shit, I had to get out of that room. Right then. But no fuckin' way was I gonna leave Shayes there. So I picked him up like I did before an' carried him into the condo.

I carried him up to the master bathroom, ran a hot tub of water an' lay him in it. An' noticed blood in the water. It seemed like an awful lot, so I checked him. Found it was comin' from his ass. Guess I *did* do some damage. Or maybe Lenny or Wayne did with some of their toys. Probably more like what those fucks'd do. Didn't matter. I only hesitated a second before I began to bathe him. I held his head up like you do a baby's an' smoothed some elegant smelly lather 'cross his chest an' down his abs an' over his pubes an' into his butt an' under his arms an' up an' down his legs. Nice legs, I remember thinkin', twenty years ago; good form to 'em — which was a fucked up thing to be thinkin' at that moment. I did it like I'd been doin' it for him all my life. Then I washed his hair with some salon shit an' rinsed it out, oh-so-carefully — didn't want any to get into his eyes. When I was done, I propped him on my lap an' used a couple of thick towels to dry him off. They were nothin' like his perfect towel an' I hated usin' 'em on him, but they were all I could find. Dunno why I did all this shit, but for some reason I...I — shit, I just wanted him clean.

I lay him on the bed then dug through Wayne's clothes, found some sweat pants an' matchin' hooded shirt, an' I slipped them on him. They were tight — which surprised me; I thought Wayne was bigger 'n that. But they fit well enough. He didn't react to anything I did. Then I left him there, in sight of the tub, an' I took a shower. A long hot shower. Keepin' an eye on him the whole time. He didn't budge.

I don't remember havin' anything like a real deliberate thought, at the time; I was still too freaked out at what I'd done. But now I can see — I know I was beginnin' to hurt for him. For what I'd done to him. They'd done to him. We'd done to him. I knew what it meant. For him. What it was gonna mean. Funny thing is, I wasn't exactly sorry that it happened. I was just sorry it had to happen like it did. If that makes sense.

No.

No, it doesn't.

It can't.

It's a crazy fuckin' thing to even think.

I taped my cut together an' wrapped a washrag to it to help stop the bleedin' before I grabbed some of Wayne's clothes. An' stopped. If they barely fit Shayes, they weren't gonna fit me. But my jeans an' shirt an' shit were all in that — that room. No choice in the matter; I needed 'em.

I wrapped a towel 'round me an' headed back down. I opened the back door an' started across the tiny-assed yard an' got up to the door. It'd almost closed so I couldn't see inside; all it'd take is a gentle push to open the door...but I froze the second I touched it. My mind was back to functionin' enough to know if I went in there I'd have to face the fact that I — I was a killer. A murderer. Times two. Yeah, yeah, I know — I did it in self-defense. Sort of. They'd have killed me if I hadn't killed them. Yap, yap, yap. I still put myself in a situation where it could've happened. No, where it was bound to happen. No excuse for that.

I was a killer.

A fuckin' killer.

Holy shit, that hit me like a ton of bricks. Lenny an' fuckin' Wayne. Dead. Murdered. By me. Aw shit, shit, shit, I never wanted anything like this to happen. Swear to God, I didn't. We were just gonna fuck with a guy who'd fucked with us. How'd it slam into such a crash an' burn?

'Cause fuckin' Wayne thought he so fuckin' smart, he could fuck with me. That's how. He thought I was just some dumb-as-dirt ex-con who didn't have a clue on how to take care of himself. That stupid — stupid-shit son-of-a-bitch. Shit.

Except he was right. I didn't know how to take care of myself. I was so full of the idea that I was in control, I lost all control. I got pulled around like some puppet who thinks it's the one decidin' where it walks an' when it talks an' how its life's gonna go. But once again, the second I thought I was makin' my own decisions an' choices, I got the rug pulled out from under an' landed square in the shit. An' now? Now I didn't know what the fuck to do.

That's when my brain shut down. Went into blank mode, again, an' gave me a breather. That's when instinct took over in a cold clear way. First off, I needed somethin' to wear. Wayne's an' Lenny's clothes'd be too small for me; shit, they were too small for Shayes, an' he's a little shorter'n I am. So I had t' get my clothes or keep the towel till I could find some someplace else.

I pushed the door open. The lights were bright an' the AC was barely keepin' the room livable. I focused on turnin' off the lights. All but one. Ignorin' the area where the bodies lay. Then I found my jeans off to one side, clear of blood. But my shirt was soakin' in it. Didn't matter; I could make do with one of Wayne's shirts. But I still took it with me. Used it to clean off my shoes. I turned the last light off an' closed the door, leavin' the AC goin'.

I snuck back to the upstairs bedroom. Shayes hadn't moved. I pulled the jeans on, found one of Wayne's t-shirts an' pulled it on. It was snug but looked like I was tryin' to show off my bod instead of just bein' too small. That'd work. I grabbed a pair of his socks an' put on my shoes. An' I was back to bein' Curt, again.

Second off, I needed to get the fuck out of there. So I gently carried Shayes downstairs an' lay him on the couch. Then pulled this throw thing that was on the back of it down over him. An' then I dug through the whole condo — every fuckin' room — lookin' for the keys to the Malibu they'd promised me. I found 'em in a side desk drawer, along with over eight hundred in cash. Which made things easier. I looked out the window. The Malibu was parked in front. There was some other shit in the joint that I knew I could hock, but I didn't feel like takin' the time.

I shoved my bloody shirt into a trash bag then peeked out

the front door to see if anything looked scary. There wasn't anybody anywhere on the street, from what I could tell. I lifted Shayes up, sort of walked him out like you'd walk a buddy who was too drunk an' got him down to the car. I sat him in the passenger seat, buckled the seat belt around him, tossed the bag of clothes in the trunk an' was about to get behind the wheel when I froze.

The tapes!

The fuckin' videotapes.

Lenny had caught it all on camera, from the point where I carried Shayes into the shed to where I killed 'em. Cops wouldn't need a confession if they saw those. Shit!

I scrambled back into the condo an' out to the shed. I almost hesitated — but I went on in, this time. I ignored their bodies an' yanked the tapes from the cameras. I did a quick once over of the room; it felt even scarier, now. An' then noticed Shayes' shredded clothes an' shoes. I grabbed them...an' finally remembered to grab his gun...an' the gym bag from the van. Jesus, that would've been a real dumb-fuck move, leavin' all that behind. I ran back to the car with everything, which joined my clothes in the trash back.

Just as I got behind the wheel, I noticed the shadows of some people approachin'. So I lay his head on my shoulder, put his hand between my legs, started the car, slipped my arm over his shoulder to pull him close an' quietly pulled away. To them — to all the world — we looked like lovers out for a drive.

It was after midnight when I turned onto Sunset.

I drove over to PCH then up to Santa Barbara. Shayes' head rested on my shoulder the whole way. We passed Zuma Beach, an' it was dark an' empty. An' I only gave a hint of a response to the memory of my first time there. That was some other century when that happened. Some other lifetime.

Anyway, the drive didn't take real long. That's the one time of life traffic moves easy in So-Cal. The night was cold an' still threatenin' rain. An' the hills ahead an' to the right were black an' the ocean on my left was stormy. An' for that hour an' a half

— maybe two hour drive...since I wasn't in a rush...I felt more at peace than I'd felt in years. He was warm beside me. Breathn' soft. Still smelled clean an' alive. I held him close as I could as I drove. Loved the weight of him leanin' against me. I almost kept goin', it was so nice. But I was back in control an' knew I couldn't.

Santa Barbara was shut down, as usual. Empty streets leadin' nowhere. All I saw for blocks an' blocks was a couple of drunk college kids an' one or two illegals headin' home on their dinky bikes. Over by the university, it was completely dead. Nothin' alive for acres in every direction.

I lay Shayes on a bus stop bench just before two. There wasn't anybody around; I made damn sure. But I heard club music playin' nearby. I hated to just dump him there, still blank an' cold an' open to get hurt, some more, an' it about to rain. So I took a book of matches, set one on fire, slipped it into the side of the strikin' area an' dropped it into a trash can, then I lit out in the car. I was two blocks away when the can started burnin'. The second I saw it, I headed for Vegas.

An' my heart ripped at me the whole way.

Chapter Eight

Man, the kidnappin' of Officer Shayes was huge fuckin' news in L-A. He *had* been missed when he didn't show up for work. They'd found his car an' the still open trunk an' the hanger of clothes in nothin' flat. In seconds, every cop in the county had been lookin' for him. Shit, every cop in So-Cal was tryin' to find out what happened. An' when he was discovered by the firemen who answered the call about a trash can fire, it got to be even bigger. 'Cause now there was a mystery involved.

I kept tabs on it from Vegas. Anything that happens in L-A is important to that town. A lot was said about how he was in a *catatonic shock*. An' how he'd been *brutalized* an' *treated viciously*. An' on an' on. But not one word about him bein' raped. I don't know if they didn't find it out when he was examined by a doctor — oh, but they must have! He was torn up pretty good; I noticed bloodstains on the Malibu's seat an' worked like a bitch to get 'em off. So maybe the cops were just keepin' it quiet, till they found out who did it. Whatever the reason, that little detail stayed out of the papers.

He *emerged from catatonia* a couple days after he was found, but his mind was blank as to what happened. Experts yammered on an' on 'bout how he just didn't *want* to remember. That his mind was blockin' something horrible. The mystery of it all — an' the fact that he was good-lookin' an' had an adorable wife an' three adorable kids — made the city go nuts. They sent him a thousand teddy bears an' ten million flowers an' started funds to help his kids through college. An' they lit candles an' held anti-violence an' *we-love-our-police* marches an' did everything they could to make him feel better. An' when he eventually wound up on disability 'cause he wasn't able to handle his duties as a cop, these same freaks paid off his mortgage an' his cars an' his credit cards an' even the hospital bills not covered by the department.

What a weird fuckin' world we live in. I couldn't get anyone, not even a fuckin' priest, to help me when I got out of County. Not one fuckin' dime's worth of encouragement. But those same fuckers did back-flips over some cop who got hurt. A homophobic prick who'd been an asshole to fags for years. If I hadn't been feelin' so confused 'bout my feelin's over Shayes, I'd of gone back an' ripped him a new one.

No.

No, I wouldn't of. Not really. Deep down, I was glad he's gettin' taken care of.

But I *was* confused. I felt towards him like I never felt towards anybody, not even Connie. It's like this — this hole was dug in behind my heart an' was layin' there empty an' I couldn't tell you why. If it was 'cause of what I'd done or 'cause of my new title in life or 'cause of all I'd lost. Or if it was just 'cause I missed the son-of-a-bitch. Shit, that couldn't be love, could it? Could I really be a fag? A homosexual. A man who loved men? I dunno. I — I still looked at women on TV like I'd like to fuck 'em. I still get the hots for this one dark-haired bitch on some comedy show I saw. Even though she's like ten years older'n me an' I really go for blonds. I even missed bein' with Connie an' wished I could find some way of gettin' back to her, even though I know it's impossible, now. She'd never put up with this shit. Never accept it. That was over an' done with, forever. But even knowin' how much I'd screwed that up, an' run Connie out of my life doin' it, I knew that hole wasn't there 'cause of it.

It was just...there.

An' I was frozen.

I'd made it to Vegas, but now I was locked in my hotel room, unable to move or sleep or even think, I was so lost. All I did was watch TV an' live off Cokes an' crackers.

As for Wayne an' Lenny, they were found a couple days later. Seems they owned this porno video store on Melrose — y'know, they never *did* tell men how they made a livin' — an' when they didn't show up to get the night's income two mornin's in a row, their manager got worried an' went over an'...well, talk about another big news item. But no one seemed to connect them with Shayes. Or me, even though now that I was thinkin', again, I was kickin' myself for leavin' behind hundreds of fingerprints an' my blood mingled with theirs an' God only knew what else.

But none of it mattered, finally. 'Cause four days later, one paper quoted the cops as sayin' there were still some other cameras in that shed. Besides the three I knew about. They were hidden in corners an' really small but still took good pictures an' got some good shots of everything that happened around that chain in the ceilin'. An' on that bed. An' that chair. An' that horse. Everything. Some of it in glorious close-up. An' that's on top of a couple of full tapes out of those cameras. Seems all I'd taken was their third load. They mentioned it to show they had some leads. But when I heard about that — shit, I knew I was done.

Sure enough, my old mug shot from Mid-State flashed onto the news the next day.

Wanted for questioning.

Person of interest.

I may be dumb, but I ain't stupid. I was stayin' in this piece of shit motel on the east side of Vegas' airport. One of those cribs where there're more bars on the windows than you find in prison. Where you know the cops'll stop by sooner or later an' the clerk'll turn you without even lookin' up from his *Playboy*.

Everything got real clear, after that. I left the motel room, bought some new clothes, then came back an' showered an' shaved. Then I went over on the strip an' had a decent meal at the Paris — my first since before that night. Then I drove back to L-A. No way was I gonna make this an *extradition* case an' add to the headlines.

I got in early — well, about ten pm. I didn't want to do

anything 'fore the eleven o'clock news, so it wouldn't make headlines till tomorrow. So I stopped near my mom's house. She was livin' in Altadena, north of the 210, with her shit of a husband. But I didn't care about that.

I was lookin' for my little brother.

Last I'd heard, he'd be graduatin' from college right around then. It'd taken him five years. Mom an' the SOB'd made him work his way through; their *real* kids took preference. I just wanted to see if he'd made it. But no way was I gonna knock on that door. No fuckin' way. So I sat there an' waited. An' hoped he'd happen to show up an' send me a sign or somethin' on how he was doin'.

Funny, my wantin' that. We'd talked about crap like that the last time I really saw him. I mean, we'd talked on the phone a couple times — when he answered it instead of my mom or the SOB. But I hadn't really talked with him since just before I was sent to Mid-State. Shit, almost eight years ago.

It was just before my trial. He was fifteen. At a bus stop, on his way home. I'd been waitin' for him, an' when he saw me drive up, he wasn't surprised.

"Hey," was all he said.

"Hey. How's it goin'?"

"It's goin'. You comin' to see mom?"

"Fuck that. I just wondered — well, you wanna grab a bite or somethin'? I'm payin'."

"Sure."

He hopped in the car an' we hit an *In an' Out Burger* just down the road. He wolfed down a double with fries an' four refills on Dr Pepper.

"Shit, don't mom feed you?" I asked.

"Healthy shit," he said with a shrug. "Crap that tastes like cardboard. But the girls love it since that's all they know."

"They'll learn. Listen, I...uh, I may be gone for a while. Three years, maybe. Dependin' on how things go." I was a real optimist, back then.

"Oh."

"Didn't want you to think I forgot you."

"You want me to come visit?"

God, he was a sharp kid. "They won't let you without mom, an' she won't let you."

"Okay. I'm sorry."

"Me, too."

We sat quiet for a while, then I asked, "How's school?"

"Okay."

"You think you'll go on to college?"

He grinned. "I'm already workin' on it. Doin' an AP." I must've given him a full blank stare, 'cause he added, "That's Advanced Placement. Good for college credit."

"Shit. You always were smart."

He shrugged. "I figured it's necessary. Sort of a preemptive strike. Mom let me know, all I'll get is room an' board if I go on. This'll cut the cost."

"Fuckin' bitch."

He shrugged.

"So you're goin' on, then."

He nodded. "I like English. Lit. I mean, all lit. Literature. I'm thinking I might write. Maybe work at a paper or some online news, something like that. Who knows?"

"You won't let nothin' stop you, right? Right?"

He just looked at me then focused on the last of his fries. They were swimmin' in ketchup in the little cardboard holder. He picked some out an' licked 'em off his fingers. An' suddenly I was hit by how good-lookin' he is. Sandy hair. Dark eyes. Clean face. Startin' to fill out, just I did at that age. All of a sudden, I hurt for him.

"I mean it. Don't let anything stop you. Not mom's shit. Not that son-of-a-bitch she married. Nothin'."

I was close to cryin'.

He looked at me. "Y'know, we're studying Russian lit. Short stories, mainly. By Chekov. He's all about man trapped in his fate, so no matter what he does, he can't escape it."

"You believe that?"

"I dunno."

"You know what I think? I think we got more control than we think. But we're too dumb or too lazy or too lost in stupid shit to see it. Me, every time I'm about to fuck up, a little bell goes off in my head an' this voice says, *don't do it*. An' every time I've done my crash an' burn, it's been when I tell that voice to fuck off. So you — you got that voice in you?"

"Sometimes."

"Listen to it."

"Okay."

"No, promise me you'll listen to it! Please! Please."

He finished his fries an' slugged down the last of his DP. "Thanks for the meal."

I knew I was pushin' too hard, so I just said, "It's nothin'."

I drove him up the hill to about a block from the house. As he was gettin' out, I said, "Y'know — you're gonna be okay."

He looked at me. "Will you?"

The question shot right through me. He's the only person who ever asked me that. The only one who ever really honestly gave a shit. An' I didn't have any answer. All I could do is shrug. He just nodded. Nothin' more to be said.

I watched him trudge up the hill to where he lived — I refuse to call that fuckin' place a home. He didn't look back. Didn't wave. Nothin'. Just walked into the house.

So there I was, just down the street, waitin' for — shit, hopin' for a final glimpse of him. Waitin' for somethin' to show me how he'd done.

Y'know, I'm not gonna bullshit anybody here 'bout how this sounds. Comin' from me. Knowin' what I've done an' how little I've fuckin' cared about the aftermath of it. But I know if anyone'd ever done to him any of the things I've done to — to some guys, I'd have killed the motherfucker. If I'd found out Wayne an' Lenny'd made him one of their boys, I'd have tracked 'em down, cut off their dicks an' rammed 'em up their asses before I slit their fuckin' throats. An' no walls could've stopped me. No cops. Nothin'. I'd felt like that about him all along, even while I was wreckin' other men's lives in Mid-state. An' after. But until this sudden fuckin' freaky connection I'd made with Shayes, I hadn't realized how — shit, just how fucked up I was to have done it. To've found reasons for it. To've excused it an' made myself feel better 'cause of it. 'Cause there were lots of other people feelin' the same way 'bout their brothers. An' sons an' friends, even. An' till I'd lost Shayes, my attitude would've been, *fuck you*. Now? Now I didn't know what the fuck to think.

A car drove up the hill. A little Mini. A cute little brunette was behind the wheel. She pulled into the driveway — an' my brother popped out of the passenger seat. An' God, he was perfect. Clean clothes, cheap but nice. Wide grin. Happy eyes. I could see 'em dancin' even from fifty yards away. He'd filled out a little; not nearly as much as me but as much as he could of, considerin' his old man was a married accountant in Minneapolis. Accordin' to my mom, that is. But the bitch might've been lyin'. An' he held himself straight. Rock solid. The girl got out an' they hugged then headed into the house, his left arm over her shoulders. An' I think I caught the gleam of a ring on his finger. I think — no, I know. I know. I know for abso-fuckin'-lutely sure it was a ring.

An' I started bawlin'.

Blubberin' like a fuckin' baby in that old Malibu. Thankin' God for how dark a night it was so my brother never could've seen me. Thankin' God he was gonna be all right. At least somethin'...somethin'...somethin' in my life was gonna be all right. Somethin'. In spite of everything. It wouldn't be perfect; I don't believe that's possible. But he wouldn't be a total fuck-up like me. Wouldn't kill anyboy's future or hopes or dreams or love or any of that shit. He wouldn't be like our mom was with us. I could see it in how he kept contact with her. Even now as he was about to start his own life. Even now that he was able to tell her to fuck off, like she deserved. Even now he could move to fuckin' Maine an' never have to see that cunt, again. He was keepin' contact with her 'cause she's his mom. Cunt that she is, she's his mom an' she's part of his life an' he was gonna make the best of it, no matter fuckin' what. An' then one day the fuckin' bitch'd see. She'd finally see how much she'd fucked up her life, too. Especially now that she's made it so perfect. She'd never admit it to me, but she might to him. An' that was good enough.

That was good enough.

It took me ten minutes to regain control.

An' when I did, I drove straight to LAPD headquarters an' turned myself in.

Epilogue

To make this already long story a little bit shorter, I got twelve-to-twenty on a plea deal. Seems the videos showed not only what I did to Shayes, but what Wayne an' Lenny did to him after I was out. Obviously out. For four solid hours. The D-A wouldn't tell me what was on 'em, but I could guess from how tight he got in his voice. An' I can't blame him for not wantin' anybody to know about that an' fuck Shayes over, even more. Plus, I know they showed me bein' raped, too, which complicated things. On top of it all, the D-A had some details he wanted kept out of the papers. Like what happened to Shayes — well, let's just say there'd been a couple of complaints filed against Wayne an' Lenny before, for — how'd they put it? *Gettin' carried away*? — with some of the guys they'd hired. An' how the cops hadn't done a fuckin' thing about it. But now they had it all on video. With sound. Glorious fuckin' sound.

Turned out the fuckers produced some of their own pornos. Bondage things. Leather. *Fantasy Fetish* shit they kept in a back room an' let only their *special* clients rent or buy. They even did some *by request* or *special order*. They had hundreds of 'em. An' there were indications that some rich fucker from Belgium or Beirut or somethin' was payin' 'em to do a queer snuff film just for him. Shit, fuckin' Wayne an' Lenny — givin' good ol' Larry Flynt a run for his money.

I didn't fight it. None of it. I took the DA's offer an' let it roll.

So now I'm back at Mid-State. An' Connie's jumped out of my life. An' it's cool. All she an' I really had in common was the fuckin'. An' now that I can get that same sense with a guy, why even ask her to stay? Not that she would've, but I think she was pissed that I didn't at least ask.

As for Mid-State, it's funny — but I do get how this place works. Get it like I never could get on the outside. Like I was born to it. Like Shamar said. An' fuckin' Chekov. An' while the guards may give me a little shit over Shayes, him bein' *a fellow cop* an' all that bullshit — as if, as regards them — it got me a huge round of respect from guys in the colony. Black, white, brown, yellow, fuckin' pink purple polka dotted — they all look at me as the guy who fucked up a cop. So I get served the best chow. I got the best cell — a two-fer even though most of the new guys are crammed into tight little four-by-fours. An' I get first dibs on the new meat — an' yes, even with all I've said, I still make use of it. It's too much a part of the reality of this place. Shit, I'm treated like a fuckin' king. An' I like the power it gives me.

An' the peace.

'Course I never told 'em a thing 'bout how I felt about fuckin' Shayes. Never will. Instead, I'm just tryin' to get the same feelin' with my new punk. An' I gotta admit, it's close. Close to the same tenderness an' compassion an' ache an' anger. This one's a nice-lookin' kid caught up in drugs — makin' cat or X or something like that an' now in for ten. He was easy to break in 'cause I don't make him do all that much. Just let me hold him. Pretend he's somebody else. I thought once or twice about fuckin' him, but I can't do that to him. Can't even make him blow me. I just have him whack me off. An' he's happy to do it. Sort of. 'Cause he's seen what happens to other guys like him then they come in here. An' he knows I can protect him. So I'll probably keep him the whole time he's in, even if somethin' better is rostered in.

An' somethin' fresh an' good is always rostered in. We got a system that thinks it's better t' put guys in jail an' let 'em become whatever they become 'stead of tryin' to help 'em stay human. How'd this one guy put it? *A survival of the fittest mentality.* I figure eventually they'll stop even offerin' probation an' just build enough jails to keep all the criminals in for the rest of their lives, no matter what they did. Saves time an' effort, in their little pea brains.

But I still gotta wonder how the hell I could let my life get so fucked up. I didn't aim to wind up here. Didn't plan to fuck myself so completely. But somehow I did one major perfect job on me. An' yeah, I may've had help along the way, but that's just an excuse. It seems like this is the only future I ever really saw for myself, an' I did my damnedest to fulfill it. An' so when you think about it that way — I got exactly what I wanted.

But you what's really funny?

I'm not sorry for it. 'Cause what I did — as fucked up as this sounds, I connected with Shayes. Somehow. Way down deep. I don't know where or why or how come or anything. I just know it brought me time with him.

An' it felt so right
when we drove up the coast
on that cold stormy night
an' for those few, few seconds
while my head felt so light
I knew deep inside
there's no reason to fight.
No reason, at all.

Yeah, I know, I know — what I did to him was rape. An' there's nothin' worse you can do to a guy. But it didn't have to be like that. Not with any of 'em. It could've been more. We could've been close. Close like I've never been with anybody, not even Connie. 'Cause I didn't really need the power. Didn't really need the control. All I really needed was somebody as strong as me who'd let me hold 'em an' be with 'em an' even lean on 'em if I needed to an'...an' why couldn't I have seen that, years ago?

Shit.

Looks like I fucked myself out of that, too.

About the Author

Kyle Michel Sullivan is an award-winning screenwriter whose sole purpose in life is to tell stories and make his characters more real than the people he actually knows. After all, only his fictional human beings can understand him and be willing to talk to him anytime he wants. He also sketches and paints and dreams of making movies out of his books.

**Books
by
Kyle Michel Sullivan**

<u>General</u>:
The Lyons' Den
The Alice '65
The Vanishing of Owen Taylor
Bobby Carapisi
Carli's Kills
A Place of Safety-Derry
A Place of Safety-New World For Old
A Place of Safety-Home Not Home

<u>Juvenile</u>:
David Martin

<u>Gay Adult</u>:
How to Rape a Straight Guy (now AKA *Curt*)
Porno Manifesto
Rape in Holding Cell 6
Underground guy
The Beast in the Nothing Room
Hunter
Blood Angel-Leonides
Blood Angel-The Prussian

Paperbacks through independent book shops and online
retailers.
E-books available through Smashwords.com

The Beast in the Nothing Room
(Sample)

Kyle Michel Sullivan

Chapter One
In the Nothing Room

Finn had no idea where he was or what had happened. One moment he was in the woods searching for poachers; the next, he was lying in a room that was dark...yet not dark, for he could see light casting a vague glow off his nose and cheeks. Both silent and not, despite an absence of sound. And it was neither warm nor cool. In fact, he couldn't even be sure it was a room because he was unable to locate any of the walls encompassing him...just like he was unable to find any source for the light shining upon him.

But what was worse? He sensed he was not alone.

He was stretched out on a bed...that wasn't a bed. It felt like there was nothing beneath him but air, simple air holding him up. He knew he was still in his clothes — a well-fitted suit in a fine modern cut, neat tie and Oxfords, completely inappropriate for tramping through the shrubs and sticks of a forest, but being a police officer, he'd had little choice.

The call had come as he was en route to Clayton-Magna to meet some friends, and the male caller's tone of voice was panicked. At least, that's what the call center had said. Strange lights whispering through the forest. Animals scattering away from it in fear. Concern it might be a drug deal going down, or what was worse...poachers. Uniforms were on their way but were fifteen minutes behind him and, since he was a Detective Sergeant, they felt he was best to at least make contact with the person reporting the incident so as to initiate a proper beginning to the investigation.

He'd agreed to do it because he didn't feel it would take too long and could hand it over to another DS, as soon as he arrived. Plus, he knew his friends would be understanding. *The life of a cop*, sort of thing. He'd made a hands-free call to Prue, the woman who'd arranged the get-together, to let her know he was running behind then turned down Mid-Clayton Road to double back for Lower Clayton-Merrill.

He gave a soft chuckle. Prue was the reason he'd worn this particular suit. It was fitted in all the right places, showing off his trim, well-formed torso and colt-like legs, though it was a bit...well...*snug* around the derriere and...um...frontal area. However, he felt very *male-model* in it, and knew she would be impressed. At least, hoped she would be. Since she was a biologist, an unspoken part of that hope was perhaps she'd also now see him as not only a prime specimen of the male figure, but a possible bed partner and, if all went well, eventual husband. He was ready to start a family, having now settled into the area and it being just past his thirtieth birthday. Find a nice cottage someplace local, somewhat similar to the Cotswold's. Not too far from the Criminal Investigations Division and DCI Blethyn, his superior. Base his life from there. They were meeting with another couple, married with a child on the way so he also hoped this was a subtle sign she might be considering him as more than a mere boyfriend. And the idea almost felt cozy and warm.

By using a bit more speed than he should have, considering the narrowness of the roads, he'd arrived to the stated location only to find...nothing. No lights. No fresh tracks from foot or vehicle. No animals, either. The forest was still and dark, despite it only beginning to approach dusk. He'd wondered if he'd gone to the wrong side, but double-checking his GPS showed he had gone to where dispatch had said.

He'd tried to go a few meters into the trees, just to get a sense of the place, but the brush was thick and he could see no path to follow. He hadn't wanted to push in too far because that would mess up his *aren't-I-hot* suit, so he was about to back away when something had struck him.

The forest was completely silent.

No sounds whatsoever.

Not even the hint of a breeze to rustle the tree branches. That had been decidedly odd, especially being this close to the Channel.

Then about a hundred meters to his left he'd seen a light. Not like that of a torch or lamp, just a soft blue glow behind the trees.

Surrounding a lone figure.

Headed towards him.

He'd jolted and begun to back away, saying, "Hello! Police. I'm Detective Sergeant Winterbourne," and the blue light had swirled around him —

And now he was here, with no idea how he got there or what was going on.

Did I fall? Knock myself out?

That had to be the explanation; the figure hadn't been close enough to reach him, and there was no indication of a weapon firing, so he'd stumbled, hit something, been struck unconscious and was dreaming. It was the only thing that could make sense.

He tried to sit up...but he couldn't move. Not his legs. Not his arms, which he finally realized were now held behind him by something that felt solid and firm, like thick cuffs. He could shift his eyes around, and could swallow, and he could breathe. That was all.

"Hello?" he called, not so much expecting an answer but only to see if he was capable of speech. He heard no echo in the chamber so figured he probably only thought he was speaking. Now he was certain he was caught in a dream.

Then he felt a whisper of air around him, like the soft caress of fingers...but nothing was there. It traced over his clean cheeks, his fine lips, his bright open eyes, a cool blue under light brown lashes. He felt it on the eyebrows he'd trimmed last night in anticipation of his date. Felt it travel through his thick curly hair, cropped close to keep from becoming too unruly. He wasn't movie-star gorgeous; he knew that, but he also knew his face was well received by most young women...and the nothing-air was touching every inch of it in ways that made him very uncomfortable.

It moved over his chin, well-shaved not an hour ago; he had issues with a light five o'clock shadow, which Prue had once mentioned in her flat Belfast brogue, and he wanted nothing that might prevent any kisses. He had even showered and changed into this suit, at the department.

He noticed the nothing-air was also caressing the back of his head and nape of his neck. Whatever it was he was lying upon made no difference; the sensations merely displaced the feeling of support momentarily as they travelled across his shoulders and down his back...then up his sides?!

What sort of dream is this?

The nothing-air in front was pacing that in the rear as it drew over his chest, tenderly exploring under his suit coat to play with his nipples. Which surprised him. He'd never had anyone finger those, before, and the fact that it sent a jolt of pleasure through him was even more startling.

Then it continued down his fairly taut abs to his groin.

He moaned with both pleasure and discomfort.

Oh...oh, no. This...this isn't real. It's all a dream.

Except it certainly felt real. Especially when the nothing-air traced over his trousers to...to fondle his crotch?!

And massage his ass?!

"What're you doing? What're you doing?!?!" he cried. Or did he merely think it? He still couldn't tell. But it had become deplorably invasive and he wanted it to stop.

After even more intimate caressing, the nothing-air traveled down his thighs and over his calves to his feet, making him cringe and try to pull away as short grunts of disbelief burst from him.

"What is this?!"

Still nothing but silence.

Then he felt the beginning of an erection.

He couldn't believe it. The nothing-air was so sensuous in its touch, he was responding?! His body was enjoying it? He was shocked beyond belief. The one positive was, he'd worn his new tight CK boxer-briefs, and those might keep him from becoming too embarrassed.

He tried to move, again, but still could not; just remained floating in the silent nothingness. He knew this was not sensory deprivation because he could see light reflecting off his face and feel himself being touched. He swallowed, fear starting to build in him.

Then he felt his shoes being untied and removed!

"Bloody hell, what're you doing?!"

No response. No echo. No proof of any sound coming from him. Just off with the shoes and a soft clunk when they dropped to the floor. Then the nothing-air caressed his soles and toes as it removed his socks, a new pair he'd worn because the only other pair that matched this suit had holes in them. Next, his suit jacket was shifted off his shoulders in soft, loving movements that were close to tenderly demanding.

"Stop! What're you doing?! I'm a police officer! Stop! STOP IT!"

His tie was undone and his shirt slowly unbuttoned.

"It's a dream, it's a dream, it's a dream, it's a dream, it's a dream," he gasped. Or maybe he was just thinking it. Hoping it. Wishing it. Because no matter how hard he tried to convince himself otherwise, he could feel every single solitary thing the nothing-air was doing. Each touch was insistent. Each caress was too real. Each movement over him was meant to lead him closer to something carnal and prurient. It didn't help that he'd been going through a dry spell and had been more than hoping Prue would take him to bed, that evening, instead of his hand being his only partner, again. But this?

This!?

Living with his grandmother...his Nan, where his mum and dad had dumped him as an infant so they could follow their own bliss...he'd had a couple of what she called *Emission Dreams*. She'd told him they were completely natural for boys hitting puberty.

"Both of your uncles went through this," she'd said, "as did your father, despite his claims to perfection. Nothing to be embarrassed about. Just make sure to give yourself a good wash." Then she'd taken his sheets and pajamas without further comment.

She'd always been the level-headed one in the family, not typically British in her understanding about sexual needs. She'd lived on a commune in Wales, traveled to Monterrey, California, and even stayed in some temple in the Himalayas for some form of awareness. All of that had carried with her, and he was glad he'd taken more after her than either of his unknown and very self-interested parents. Remembering this helped calm him and let him focus on the reality of the moment.

As soon as he could figure out what that reality was.

To start with, he knew this could not be happening except in his mind. So no matter what the nothing-air did, it wasn't real. It couldn't be. Despite what his body was telling him.

That helped when the nothing-air pulled his shirt open to reveal his undershirt — tight, white, and just a little see-through — then slipped the crisp cotton down and off his arms with a touch that was almost worshipful in its caress. The shirt was softly whispered past his hands even though they were still caught behind him...which made no sense, but that was the reality of this dream.

His breath was coming faster as he fought to keep panic at bay, and his well-formed pecs were causing the undershirt to shift a little over his now tender nips. He was proud of how he'd built himself up, after having been born underweight and sickly, and it seemed the nothing-air agreed, because it ran over his muscles and fondled and flicked and twisted his nipples through the fabric, making them tent against the light cotton, every touch shooting fire into his groin. He was in shock at how lovely it felt. How fantastic it was. How he didn't want it to stop. How a tingle behind his balls was actually making him groan from pleasure.

Christ, is this what I want Prue to do to me?

Then the nothing-air ripped his undershirt open to reveal his smooth, barely tanned skin was laced with a dash of tawny hair that swirled down his abs to his groin. He yelped as the caresses ran across his belly and over his shoulders and along his arms to guide the shirt's remains away in ways that seemed to sear the heartbreaking prurience of its touch into his very soul.

His breath grew sharper. Heavier. Was punctuated with grunts of fear. He fought to keep one thought in his mind.

It's NOT real, Finn, it's not real, it's not real.

But he was losing the battle. The sensations brought on by the nothing-air were too demanding. Too consistent. And on top of it, his dick was growing fat and hard, in response.

Even though he could not move his torso or arms or legs.

Just an emission dream, that's all, just an emission dream.

Then his trousers were unbuttoned!

He fought to picture Prue being the one doing it. Picture how lovely she was. Round in all the right places. Peaches and cream skin under golden red hair cut just right. That Belfast brogue. He'd been attracted to her the second he met her on a murder case. She'd been a suspect, for a little while, so their beginning had been tainted by that, but it was Blethyn who'd made the accusations, not him. After some stumbling, he'd been able to get her to know him and let him know her, and now...well...using the image of her helped him refocus and make this nightmare into something he could handle. If he was going to be dream-mauled, sexually, at least it would be by someone he wanted.

His zipper was lowered, almost teasing, and his trousers were guided past his hips and rear with the same tenderness and beauty as was done with his shirt. And under those briefs, he was totally ready to go. The nothing-air danced back up to play with his dick and balls through the cotton, not only whispering around them and over them and under them and along them but making the taut material surrounding them feel like something alive and needy. It also massaged the cheeks of his ass as if they were ripe melons. He didn't have a bubble-butt, but it was a nice size and fit him just right. Apparently the nothing-air agreed, for this continued as his trousers were maneuvered down his legs to his ankles while the caresses wafted over the soft down on his thighs and calves. The elegant sensations were beginning to overpower his ability to concentrate.

Then the waistband of his CKs was grabbed...and they were pulled down to his ankles, where his trousers waited, exposing an erection that may not be the biggest dick ever but was certainly above average. At least, none of the women he'd been with had complained. He'd even caught a few lads in the gym casting him glances of either envy or interest, or both.

But now?

Like this?

As he was being violated?

The trousers were gently removed, then off went the CKs with even more caresses over his calves.

And he was now completely naked.

Completely vulnerable as the dreadful intimacy continued.

I'm handling it. I'm handling it.

Then the nothing-air slipped between the cheeks of his ass and touched his rectum.

"NO! STOP! THIS ISN'T RIGHT! YOU CAN'T DO THIS!" he screamed.

He fought to squirm away but his body still would not move. His breath was fast and furious, and while he could shift his eyes to look around and move his mouth to speak and knew damn well he really was yelling and snarling words into the nothingness, he also knew his nips had grown pointy and his balls were happily being juggled and his dick was being stroked while every other part of his body was also being mauled.

Bloody hell. Is this an alien abduction? Are those bloody

stories true? No, I have to be hallucinating. I have to be!

Now the nothing-air danced over his nips to send more lightning through every nerve in his body. Caressed the hair on his abs and wandered through his pubes like they were rafting down a river that cascaded into gentle pond. Glided over his ass. Fondled his dick and balls in ways that seemed more like worship than sexual need. Sensations swirled up and down his thighs and calves, adding to the build of erotic need within him.

His dick was now as hard as it had ever been, and he was whimpering at the incessant manipulation of it taking him almost over the edge...but never quite. Stroking. Caressing. Loving it. Holding it straight up so that he could just see the head of his penis if he looked down with his eyes. He felt some form of covering glide over it, like a condom, but so far as he could tell nothing was actually being put on him.

"No, no, no, no..." was all he could murmur, now. He knew his cries and screams and pleading would do no good, but they still jolted from him at each step in the invasion.

Then a form appeared in the dark space above him, shining so bright he had to jam his eyes closed. As he adjusted to its glow, he slowly realized this was another man. Also naked. Lean and tightly muscled, with dark fans of hair over his body in all the places it should be. Nearly black eyes under thick lashes. A two-day growth of beard on his strong chin, surrounding full lips. A couple years older. He saw the hair on the man's body shift slightly, as if he, too, were being caressed.

And he was also sporting an erection, his shaft ripe, his knob red, his foreskin drawn completely back from the head.

The suddenness of it jolted Finn, and jammed one thought into his mind.

I know him. I know him. From where?

The man recognized him, as well. His expression shifted to confusion. Then shock.

"Him?" the man said, in a Geordie accent. "It's him?! No!"

"Newcastle!" Finn said, in shock. "You...uh, you're Hallsworth! Detective Inspector...uh, Joss Hallsworth?"

The man's expression grew pained he said, "Yeah. I know you. Winterbourne, from down South. Conference a few years back, at New Scotland Yard. You'd just gained Detective Sergeant."

"Right, right. What the hell's going on!?"

Joss almost laughed. "If I could explain it, I would. How'd they trap you?"

"Trap? I...I...I got called out to investigate some lights. Caller said...well, he thought they were...uh...they were..."

"Poachers," said Joss. "Bloody hell..."

"No argument there," Finn said...then felt the nothing-air slip up against his anus and he cried out, in shock. "STOP IT!"

"They're all over you. Right?"

Finn had to fight a panic building in him. "I...I'm...I'm dreaming you?"

"No. You're not." His voice sounded mournful. "I...bloody fuckin' hell, not him! Not him!"

Not him?

The nothing-air pushed harder against Finn's rectum. He fought to keep from screaming then gasped, "What do you mean? Are they mauling you, too?"

"This is how they work. Touch and grope and fondle and abuse...and...and nothing's there."

"That's what they're doing to me, but I can't move and...and..." Finn's nips were pinched, making him shout, "WHO THE BLOODY HELL ARE YOU? WHY'RE YOU DOING THIS?"

Then Finn realized he wasn't lying down; he was upright, as was Joss. And they were closer together. Closer. Closer. Until their erections touched each other. Slipped side by side. Held in place as the nothing-air whispered over the both of them. Fondled them, together. And it felt so good...too good...too damn good.

"STOP! STOP IT!" Finn cried. "This is rape!"

"Oh, Christ," Joss said, "I can't...please...not him..."

Finn focused on Joss. "What're you saying?!"

"They're using me. Against you. Against others. Take me whenever they want and...no, don't make me do it, not to him! Please..."

Finn felt the nothing-air surround his ankles and lift his legs up and up, even as his arms remained locked behind him and the caresses and the probing continued all over him.

He screamed, "NO! YOU'RE NOT — YOU CAN'T — NO! THIS IS RAPE! THIS IS RAPE!"

"They don't care," Joss murmured. "They don't follow our laws. Dammit, don't make me, please, not him."

The nothing-air rested Finn's legs on Joss's broad shoulders, his ass now completely open and vulnerable. Then he felt Joss's erection press against him.

"Finn, I'm sorry..."

"NO, NO, NO, NO, NO!"

The nothing-air opened Finn's cheeks wider.

Joss's dick pushed in.

Finn howled in pain.

It kept going in. Slowly. Slowly. Filling him. Deeper and deeper. He felt he was being torn in half and yelled and snarled in anger and frustration. And still he could not move to get away from it.

"I'm sorry, Finn, I'm sorry, I'm so sorry..."

Then Joss's erection was all the way inside, right to the base; Finn could feel the man's pubs against his skin. He felt the covering over his dick begin to pulse up and down, stroking him as Joss began rocking in and back and in and back and in and back.

I'm getting wanked as he buggers me?!

Finn gasped harsh and fast. His eyes slammed shut and he howled. He felt the nothing-air pinch his nips and whisper over his pecs and caress his thighs and toy with his pubes and fondle his balls as the unseen covering stroked his dick, making it harder and harder and bringing it closer and closer to the brink then stopping just before he could let go then starting, again, and it went on and on and on and every push in hurt and every pull back was like fire and he screamed and yelled and cursed and tried to fight but couldn't move as he was mauled and groped and felt up and fucked and pulled at and it kept on and on and on and then...then slowly...oh so slowly...almost exquisitely, to his shock, the pain shifted...and each thrust began to feel like something beautiful and wanted and every nerve in his being was filled with pleasure. Each stroke on his own dick made it grow even harder. His balls became even more tender and quivered each time Joss's pubes brushed against them. His nips were crazed by each light lovely pinch. His calves and thighs laughed with joy from the nothing-air traveling over them. He couldn't believe it.

I'm enjoying being fucked by a man I barely know!? Getting off on being raped?

In and back and in and back, over and over and over, each thrust taking him closer and closer to a stunning nirvana. The passionate demands of it finally enveloped him and he lost all sense of time or reality as Joss kept going in and back and in and back and kept on and on and on for hours and hours and Finn didn't care because he wanted it and needed it and hoped it would never end.

Until he felt a rush build from behind his balls and roll through his body as every muscle in him clenched and joined with the nothing-air's caresses to make him grunt and let out a bellowing roar as the rush slammed down his thighs and across his ass and over his nips and up into his dick and a massive line of cum exploded from him, the like of which he had never experienced. It vanished into the invisible covering as he fired again and again and again, each jolt better than the last, draining him of what seemed like gallons of semen.

Then Joss slammed harder and harder against him and jolted and shuddered and stopped deep inside and cried out...and filled him with his own cum. Gasping and whimpering in both pleasure and horror and joy and pain, he rammed against Finn harder and harder, sending more and more flooding into him. On and on until he was a quivering, laughing mass and could make nothing in the way of a coherent sound.

Finn was so lost in his own overwhelming sensations and feelings and exultation, he was just as incoherent.

After what seemed like hours but was probably only a few minutes, stillness returned to them both and Finn slowly...slowly...slowly drifted back to himself. He found he was able to move his head, now. His arms hung limp, behind him. He looked at Joss, whose eyes were half-closed, his face slack from the intense pleasure as he pulled out. His dick was still dripping with semen.

No condom on him.

Finn's own dick lay back on his belly, fat and clean and satisfied with itself. He was even still erect. Somewhat. And he felt nothing surrounding it, anymore, as it began to shrink back to normal. Then his legs were removed from Joss's shoulders.

The man looked at him, confused.

"You're still here," he whispered, a near smile on his face. "Still here. You're not...not..."

"What...you mean?" Finn managed to gasp.

Joss cast Finn a vague, sorrowful glance as he murmured, "They. They made me. Do this. To others. So many others. Just like us. Till they. Till they let loose, same as you. They all did. But they. They left. Fell away. You haven't. Now I see. So sorry."

"Were you...done like this, too...?"

"I...I'm so sorry. Didn't want this. For you. Sorry."

"Not your fault," Finn murmured.

Joss smiled. "That's what. Rob said. Manchester's finest, he was. Poor bastard."

Then Joss drifted back into the blue light.

Finn felt the nothing-air still caressing him. Fondling him. Probing him. Nips, balls, dick, thighs, ass, back, sides, face, feet...but it was in a manner that seemed sweet and caring. Loving, even.

Which made no sense. Did his assailant think he'd been made love to? Had this really been some bizarre alien abduction and the bastards believed it was a proper sexual coupling of Earth people? That he'd wanted it to happen? Despite his screams and struggles? It had hurt like hell, and he was brutally sore from the fucking...but he had to admit how mellow and easy he felt after having cum like he did. So much so, he almost didn't care about being violated.

That shocked him more than anything — the idea that he had rather enjoyed being raped by Joss!

In his head, he knew this had been a harsh, vicious, cruel, manipulative, painful sexual assault. But a deeper truth also made itself known.

I want it to happen, again.

His unbelievably intense ejaculation at the end of it had overcome the horror of everything else. He felt like someone coming down off his first snort of coke, who wanted more, wanted to regain that high. It frightened him, but also put him at ease.

Which makes absolutely no sense whatsoever.

He felt his CKs being slipped back up his legs in gentle caresses. The tight, white cotton softly surrounded his ass and scrotum as the nothing-air adjusted his dick and balls so he was comfortable. Next came his trousers, socks and shirt, followed by his shoes. The tie was knotted around his neck, and the suit coat came on and the light swirled blue and —

He was lying in the forest, two constables watching over him, one young and fit, the other older and more concerned. The young one was on a mobile phone.

"'E's coming 'round, sir," the man said. "Yes, still needs a medic. 'E looks pretty shaky."

Finn made himself sit up, even though he felt rather dizzy. He glanced at the fit young constable and noticed how the lad completed that uniform very nicely, in every way, his pale blond hair, chiseled features, and strong tanned forearms glistening with golden down adding to his beauty.

Confused, Finn had to make himself look away.

"How long?" he murmured, his voice shaky.

"We got here 'bout twenty minutes, ago, sir," said the older constable. "Saw your car and looked around. Couldn't find you till there was some lightning in the clouds and I noticed you here. Dunno why we didn't see you, before. I loosened your tie."

"Know what 'appened?" the young constable asked.

Finn shook his head and started to get up. The older man held him down.

"I'd stay put, were I you, sir. That's a nasty cut over your ear."

Finn touched a sore spot behind his right ear and his fingers came away with dabs of blood on them. He sighed. So it was all just a dream. He was only sore from having fallen or been hit; he wasn't sure which, yet.

Which was vaguely disappointing.

He almost laughed. He'd never even thought of being with a man, before, let alone getting buggered by one, but here he was, sad that what had happened in his head hadn't occurred in reality. It was madness.

But something didn't add up. He ached in every part of his body, as if he'd overdone his workout, something he never did. Could that be from just a blow to the head? And should his ass hurt like he'd taken a really hard bowel movement? And his nipples, why were they so tender? And why did he feel so...so different, now, as if his whole world had shifted?

That's when he realized his undershirt was gone.

I always wear one.

A weird sort of relief swept over him and he smiled. It really had happened. He felt his balls tingle and his dick shift in agreement, and with it came a surprising hunger. An odd sort of need.

And that lovely young constable would be just the tonic for it.

A thousand questions exploded through Finn's mind. One moment he's dreaming of a night with a beautiful woman; the next, he's focused on the very nice rear and well-formed legs of a man and thinking how much he'd like to have access to them?

Really?

So was he queer, now? Had the aliens made him a poof? One of his uncles was gay, and he was the coolest man Finn had ever known. Had he decided to swing to that side, thanks to this?

No, the very idea was ridiculous. One doesn't go gay from a smack to the head, and you can't rape a man into changing his sexual orientation. The whole process would be too traumatic.

The thing was, he didn't feel traumatized. Which made even less sense. He had dealt with rape victims when he was a constable, and there had always been a sense of powerlessness and trauma and anger and pain, involved. Why not with him?

It looked like Prue would have to wait, because he needed to sort this out, and the first step towards doing that would be to track down Joss. Find out what he knew about this whole mess. If he had any form of an explanation. Then would come finding what sounded like a fellow officer named Rob. *Manchester's finest*, as Joss put it. Finn needed to see if his reactions had been the same as his own. If his world had been shifted as much. He bet Rob would turn out to be someone about the same age and as fit as him and Joss.

Poor bastard, Joss said. Perhaps a DS like me, whose world's shifted, too? Confused, too?

Finn began to smirk at the thought. For some reason, he wanted to spend as much time as possible with Rob. To compare notes, of course. Support each other. See if they could figure out why this happened. Maybe they could even sequester themselves in his gay uncle's B&B, near Whitford Park.

For a long leisurely weekend. In a double bed. Engorging on carry-out...and the pleasure of his company. Uncle Niall wouldn't mind.

That thought brought an even more-wicked gleam to Finn's eye. Then he and Rob could go to Newcastle and face down Joss, together. Something about the man's careful choices of words and reticence in answering Finn's questions made him fairly certain there was more going on than he was saying. Especially taking into account how he'd danced around the comment of having been used in the same way as them.

Whatever had happened, they needed to dig up the reason they both had been taken, and why a man like Joss was the one doing the taking. Finn remembered he had a wife and kids. Of course, that didn't mean much; Joss could be bisexual. So they would need to guide him away from the family. To a hotel, maybe. Where they could pick his brain and drag more about the other rapes from him. He had indicated there were others, hadn't he? Other men brutalized like them.

Which sent a shiver diving straight into Finn's scrotum.

He almost hoped Joss would not be forthcoming about the other men.

Wasn't that a cute choice of words?

But it could give him and Rob *justification* to introduce their *unwilling rapist* to the joy of being on the receiving end. Show him what he'd missed by not being used like them.

Get some of our own back. Wouldn't that be fun?

Finn jolted.

A detective Sergeant as sensible and sure as he was, who knew right from wrong, without question, considering breaking a dozen sexual assault laws, *fun*?

What the hell had happened to him? Finn was not a believer in alien abductions, but something ridiculously confusing and intense had taken hold of him and he had no other rational explanation for it. All he knew for certain was, his whole way of viewing sex had been altered, and he now felt not only different and confused but also delightfully dangerous.

He heard sirens approaching. One of them an ambulance. He touched the injury behind his ear. The blood was already coagulating, and he felt no real pain. No headache. Nothing but a soft murmur of a throb. Could that have been the cause of his shift in perceptions? Did something like this happen after a concussion? Should he see a specialist to make certain he wasn't damaged more than he thought?

Yes, that had to be it. He'd been assaulted and struck unconscious, and it had scrambled his brain. He was just thinking he'd worn an undershirt, because he always did, but might not have had a clean one to change into after his shower. Of course. It all made sense, now. He'd probably feel back to normal once he'd had a checkup and good night's sleep.

Except...

A singular thought insisted on bouncing around in his mind.

Me and Rob on Joss. Yes, that would be fun.

And not one iota of his being even considered rejecting the idea.